*Books By*

# Drew and David VanDyke

## SUPERNATURAL SIBLINGS SERIES

*MoonRise - Book One*

*MoonFall - Book Two*

*BloodMoon - Book Three*

Visit our website at:
**www.davidvandykeauthor.com**

BLOODMOON
Copyright © 2015 by Drew VanDyke and David VanDyke
All Rights Reserved.
Printed in the United States of America.

Published by Reaper Press

ISBN-13: 978-1-62626-187-7

ISBN-10: 1-62626-187-3

# BLOODMOON

## Supernatural Siblings Series
### Book Three

Drew VanDyke

and

David VanDyke

# Acknowledgments from Drew

This book is dedicated to all of those affected by the fire that swept through Middletown, California in September 2015, and destroyed lives and livelihoods in the area surrounding Harbin Hot Springs.

For Cullen, Ganymede and Warren: A guy couldn't ask for a better set of packmates.

Thanks to Dave and Beth for your continued love and support and for giving me a home away from home. And for Dad, Conda, Leslie, Phaedra, Bryson, Spanky and Sebastian. It just wouldn't be Knightsbridge without you.

# -Prologue-

*Growing up, our older brother Adam used to call us twins "a walking sideshow on four legs." Now I walk on four legs all by myself.* – Ashlee Scott

Dear Diary:

Yes, it's true.

Will is a werewolf.

At least he will be once the full moon hits for the first time.

We've been trying to prepare him. Well, Jackson and Sully have. I found out early in life that friends and family are sometimes the last people I want to teach – or learn from, for that matter. So, I let the guys do their thing.

They've taken him out with Luken and Elka and he's been studying up on wolf facial expressions. I guess it's like learning sign language. It's one thing to learn how to sign, but it's a whole 'nother ball game learning how to read signs coming at you from the other direction. Anyway, I'm hoping that once he turns, it will all fall into place, because frankly his anxiety right now is working my edges.

Since he took the bite, he's been super moody. Eats more voraciously than before and growls at other guys who even look in my direction. I think Jackson and Sully are pulling his chain in the comport-yourself-like-a-werewolf department, but he is getting awfully interested in smelling everything, including my underwear...but maybe all guys do that. Do they?

Anyway, I guess he's all in. But I'm not sure if he knows what he's all in for. I mean, what if after a few years of my kind of crazy he decides he isn't into putting up with all of my shit? Am I up for a round of heartache if he decides to walk away? Not to put the kibosh on anything, but I've seen friends split up and it looks incredibly painful.

Anyway...Ghost Mom just told me to hang on to my hat, because my life is only going to get weirder, before it, er, well...doesn't.

Yippee-ki-yay...never mind.

Now for this next bit I'm sure you'll wonder why I'm telling you all this stuff about Con Shelby. Heck, I'm a writer. It's what I do, taking notes and interviews and recollections and trying to fit them into a coherent whole for your enjoyment...because real life never makes as much sense as a good story.

And what's life without a good story, anyway?

\*\*\*

Constantine Andronicus Shelby hovered above his Knights-bridge Canyon, California territory and surveyed the demesne he'd been assigned. It wasn't easy bringing a new location under the jurisdiction of Council authority. With the lycanthropes interested in repopulating the area

with wolves and the witches demanding more represent-
tation, they needed his steady presence to maintain the
magical status quo.

Con shifted from owl to coyote form and meandered
along the back trails of the canyon, re-enchanting the
marker stones that both warned and warded the area
against unwanted supernatural intrusion. He lifted his leg
on each to remind the mated pair of natural wolves
Jackson and his pack had brought into the area that these
stones defined the limits of his influence.

The Montana Grade Wolves had arrived on schedule,
and aside from a few minor issues with some local wild
talent, had settled in nicely. Well, perhaps the issues
weren't so minor, but Con was determined to make them
so. During his last century of wandering, he'd come to
believe that an important part of ruling effectively was
knowing what was beneath his notice, what to pay
attention to and what to ignore.

Stirring the pot often ruined the stew, as his sire had
once told him, and a peaceful demesne was a happy
demesne.

And Con appreciated his own happiness as much as
any immortal.

A vampire was like a landholder, he mused. The
supernatural denizens were his vassals, whether they knew
it or not. The animals of the night – the bat, the owl, the
rat, the cat – were his eyes and ears, and the wolves, being
pack animals and by temperament more amenable to
leadership, were his enforcers. It had always been this way
– vampire and wolf in alliance, protecting a territory and a

secret, policing themselves and with deadly efficiency dealing with those who broke the conventions.

Finished with his chore, Con shifted into a thick charcoal vapor that whirled and swirled, a splash of paisley against a painted fabric sky. The dark slipstream of the vampire's passing slashed toward the lights of the twinkling city below.

The town of Knightsbridge had lain blanketed in a supernatural muffling for decades. Churches on every corner and the piety of the faithful meant that incarnations of the Goddess in the town were usually limited to manifestations of the Blessed Mother. Other practitioners, such as the Street Witches and those who met regularly at the White Rabbit for lunch had struggled, inhibited by the disapproving atmosphere.

This lack of an embodied imagination regarding the Divine Feminine meant that Knightsbridge had been uninviting to most supernatural types until recently, when a new generation of its children, raised on social media, told stories of the town's idyllic allure, putting the Knightsbridge Canyon area on the popular map once more.

Too quickly, the nearly forgotten Coventry of Knightsbridge became inundated with wealthy transplants from the chilly Bay Area or congested Los Angeles, seeking the perfect California combination of climate, natural beauty and upscale cuisine. With them came jobs and the people to fill them, and naturally, not everyone was mundane.

For the vampire community, all of this meant the place was finally worth appointing a master, and Con was the first since the bust of the Gold Rush of 1849 made it all but a ghost town.

Survey complete, his misty foot touched down at the base of the canyon and he strode onto the safety of his own estate, his form solidifying into an alabaster idol of chiseled flesh, his lean musculature ashen, drawn and tight with the absence of fat.

*Must feed.* His innards growled at him, the result of the exertions of repeated shifting and the enchantments he'd performed.

The more sated a vampire was, the more color he retained and the better he could pass for a mundane human. When his well of blood ran dry, he took on a chalky appearance and might be mistaken for a marble statue.

He disappeared into the Victorian gothic structure of the old wood-and-stone rectory, his abode nestled in the velvet woods past Knightsbridge Commons, and left a parted group of fireflies bobbing to light the remnants of his presence as he prepared for the day.

Con opened his double-wide stainless steel refrigerator door, grabbed a plastic blood bag and sucked it down, wrinkling his nose against the unpleasant cold. He put up with it for the sake of his thirst as a mundane might have drunk yesterday's stale coffee to clear his head. It didn't take long for his reflection to take on the pink glow of humanity.

Next stop was his expansive, well-equipped bathroom, and he reveled in the modern convenience of indoor plumbing as the hot water of the steaming shower washed the remains of his nocturnal prowling down the drain.

Once finished, he called for those intimates on duty –
even thralls needed days off, after all – and took and gave
pleasure, feeding on their warm *vitae* as a gourmand might
sup at a fine table.

Later, at his dressing table, he glanced in the mirror at
himself and chuckled at the old superstition about
vampires. There was magic in the world, but it was
practical, sensible, and it conformed, more or less, to the
constraints of physics. When it didn't, the cost to the user
was quite high.

Clothing himself in the conservatively tailored gar-
ments of a successful businessman, he ran his hands
across the soft-as-butter fabric of his white silk shirt,
brushed navy trousers and mustard-colored waistcoat,
smoothing away the wrinkles and adding a bronze pocket
watch and chain to tie up the look.

He wasn't a tall man, but he had a presence about him
borne of confidence in his power and authority. Clear
spectacles and a coat of silver at his temples and brow
made him appear to be in his mid-forties, with salt
and pepper hair, a cross between Doctor Strange and
Doctor Who.

Once he'd brushed his teeth – one couldn't be too
careful with them, after all – they shone with a whiteness
even greater than his fair skin, and he practiced his smile
in the mirror, making sure to call up an internal emotional
reality that reached his eyes. It was an actor's trick, an
illusion that served him as he looked forward to bringing
this land to heel.

It also served his continued dalliance with the lady Margaret Stenfield, a widow and mother of two, grandmother of one. He stopped by his bedroom where she lay, still asleep, and kissed her forehead. She stirred, but didn't wake. His code, his sense of *noblesse oblige* and responsibility for his vassals – what substituted for morality in his unbeating heart – was fulfilled by the good he was doing for her.

It didn't hurt that his paramour was mother to the lupine girl's lycanthrope lover, which allowed him to keep an eye on those two through the relationship. As with everything Con did, pragmatism figured prominently.

Thus far, his accomplishments this first year had made him content, if not entirely happy. Resolving to continue his improve-ments until everything fell into place, he made his way to the garage and the sleek silver Mercedes with tinted windows.

The people of Knightsbridge demanded he look the part, and unknowingly became sheep to his shepherd, the wolves serving as his sheepdogs to watch the flock.

Flocking sheep. He smiled at the image and drove across town to his place of business, the Grand Illusion Magic and Curio Emporium, arriving before the sun crested the horizon.

Inside, he greeted Edward, his day manager, and allowed the man to fill him in on the significant events of yesterday: who came in, what they bought, what they might be interested in acquiring. The shop provided Con a cover for his evident wealth and status, and its uniqueness and selection of antiques ensured that most of the upper crust of Knightsbridge – the people who mattered, anyway – visited from time to time. This was one way he kept his finger on the pulse of the mundanes and picked up tidbits about more important matters.

As he had been a competent stage magician in his former life, the shop also allowed him to keep in touch with that part of him-self. He'd been performing shows at the university each semester, open to the public, to stay in practice and to provide a further entry into society.

Flipping the door sign to *OPEN*, Constantine Shelby took a deep, unnecessary but contented breath, and prepared for his usual short morning's presence before returning to his abode to sleep away the greater part of the day.

"So, when are you going to give up the condo in the city?" Amber asked as we sat dipping scones in honey-butter and sipping what I called "froufrou" coffee on the patio, and watching an abnormal summer rain and fog sweep through the canyon one Saturday morning when the rest of the family was still asleep.

Amber was bundled up in a grey and pink bebe number on the outdoor sofa while I looked more like Old Navy crossed with Girls Fight Club in green plaid boxers and a black wife-beater on the chaise lounge.

Hey, I was at home. Who was I supposed to impress? Besides, it felt really good to hang out with my twin sister, no more than the usual tension between us, like a return to old times. I guess it was because the biggest secret between us, about me being a lupine, was no longer hidden.

"How did you know I was thinking about...?" My voice trailed off. "Never mind."

We were doing that thing we often do when we're alone together, talking but not looking at each other. Because frankly, watching the emotions that played across my sister's face during a conversation, the downside of being an identical twin and knowing each other so well, made me pick up and subconsciously assume her state of being. I had enough of my own crazy to deal with without adding Amber's to the mix.

"Ashlee, it makes no sense to keep paying rent on a place you haven't been to in how many months?"

"I have a friend staying there," I said. True, my friend Xiana was only paying half the rent, but I was *so* not going to tell Amber that or I'd get a lecture on money management and how not to get taken advantage of. "And it's only till my lease is up and then I can walk away free and clear."

"I still think you could have gotten out of there sooner."

I quoted Dad at her. "Yeah, well hindsight is better than foresight."

She growled, but said nothing. I was seriously starting to wonder who was the werewolf around here. Before you know it the whole family was going to be barking at each other. Hell, we were already barking mad.

"And, how's Peg doing?" Amber asked. "Last time I saw her she was looking fairly fragile. You said it was what, stage four cancer? That poor family."

"Oh, I guess I didn't tell you." I began, but she interrupted.

"So, is she? Like, dying?"

"No, she's in remission."

"How'd that happen?" My sister turned to gaze directly at me.

I watched what I call her "mind-reading frown lines" appear. I wanted to tell her to please stop making me look like that, but she wouldn't find it funny, so I gave her the short version on Con and Peg.

"Wow, you *have* been keeping secrets," my twin said and pursed her lips in disapproval. "So is she going all vamp on us, or what?"

"Not as far as I know. As long as she continues to take Con's blood, regular ingestion keeps her suspended in a sort of half-life, but without a bunch of mumbo jumbo she doesn't turn into a vampire either. I don't know. I couldn't do it."

"You're not a mother."

Amber bit her lip as I flared up at her. "You know, I'm getting really sick of you throwing that in my face, considering..."

"Upside, at least now you don't have to cheat on Will with a gay guy to make your super-pups and save the planet," she interrupted, throwing me off my game.

"I'm not saving the planet," I growled at her and finished to myself, *just this little part of it.*

"So, how's Will holding up?"

"Besides a lot of anxiety, at least when I'm around, I think he's enjoying his bromance with Jackson and Sully. Maybe too much. If he's not growling at the straight guys he's woofing at the gay ones. I know it's something that even canines do, but I am *so* going to beat Jackson down for teaching him that one."

"Yeah, make sure he chills out before the holidays arrive. Elle and I do have straight friends you know, with husbands."

"Believe me, if he doesn't, I'm going alpha on his ass and he'd better bare his throat to me."

"Next MoonFall's what? A week away?"

"Yeah. I was thinking about heading up to Harbin or maybe the city, I don't know. Darla and Twyla are doing Laguna Del Sol."

Amber made a face and I smelled her displeasure. She was so not into nudist resorts like the rest of us. But when you're a werewolf, do as werewolves do.

"We all thought it would be better if there were no bitches around during Will's first turn," I continued. "Hopefully he'll get whatever he needs to out of his system because the following MoonFall we're installing Jackson as Alpha of the Knightsbridge Canyon territory. Doggie dignitaries, yea."

"How's that going to work anyway? Since Will's going to father the wolf pups, you would think he would take over as Alpha, but I can't see that happening."

"Oh, well, Jackson is going to forego his right for the night of the Blood Moon and when the cubs are born we'll be turning them over to the ulv to raise."

"How do you feel about that?"

"You *so* do not get to shrink me on this one."

"Well, if it's not me, I hope you're talking to someone."

I was. But I was talking to Ghost Mom and I didn't want to rub in the fact that Amber couldn't see her and I could. We still hadn't resolved our last debacle of an argument over mom's presence in our lives, but I think

Amber caught it anyway, because she got this pained look on her face. "You would think with your kind of crazy you would be trying to simplify your life, not complicate it. So, when do you think you're going to have them? The pups, I mean."

"I was thinking about sticking to a normal schedule. Wolves generally breed during the winter so they can give birth in the early spring."

"Really? That's like, right around the corner."

"But Blood Moons only happen once or twice a year. There's about six months between. So, I was thinking about waiting a year. Give Will time to get acclimated to his new lifestyle."

"Lifestyle? Ugh. I hate that word. Dad used to use that term to describe Elle and me. A lifestyle is about what kind of wine you like, not about sexual preference. Otherwise I'd have to ask when the all shifters around here are coming out of the closet. Because that's gotta be a new minority frontier. Puts a new L in LBGTQIA…are there any more letters lately?"

I stuck my tongue out at her and she reached over with her pointer finger and touched it, zapping me.

"Ow!" I said around a mouthful of numb-tongue. "How'dyoudothath?"

"It's a secret," she said and she left me silent as she answered her phone, which had begun to ring.

When she came back, Amber said, "Well, that was weird."

I gave her the "continue" sign.

"Rhonda wants to come visit over Halloween."

"That's not like Dad. He hates Halloween. Especially Halloween in Knightsbridge."

"No, not Dad. Just Rhonda."

"Really, what for?"

"She swore me not to tell Dad, but she's coming for a convention."

"Huh."

My sister momentarily put on her City Manager's Department hat. "Ashlee, the only convention in Knightsbridge over Halloween is for the Street Witches."

"Since when is Rhonda interested in small town neighborhood watches led by people who want to keep downtown tourism viable and cruising Main Street safe for their teenagers?"

"You might as well know." Amber looked around as if making sure nobody could hear us. "Though the Street Witches is a real community organization, a number of them are also real witches. The charity work happens, but it's also a cover for the Wiccans, the Goddess Worshippers and the Magick practitioners in our midst. Elle and I have been assigned to provide oversight. We're bringing in Adam's firm for security, too."

"But that means?"

"Our stepmother's straying from the party line, which would be to have nothing to do with people like that."

"What? No, really? " No wonder she wants to keep her interest from my Dad. "Didn't see that one coming."

Now, let me tell you about our father's wife.

Rhonda came into our lives after all the kids were grown. It was eight or nine years after Mom's death and

Dad had begun dating again, to mixed results I might add, after year five.

So, when he went looking for a new life-mate while Amber went to college and I bummed around Europe for a year, he wasn't looking for a mom for his children. He was looking for a help-meet, as the Bible says. Which is great, because Rhonda loves him and wants to make him happy. Us? Not so much. While she has exquisite taste for her demographic and despite the overabundant love for all things pueblo, she isn't the easiest person to be around.

And...up until this point, I'd never seen her take any initiative. She usually followed my father's lead – and in Dad's world, God is a dude, all three pieces. Father, Son and Holy Spirit. Not *The Dude*, of course.

Back in high school I'd once postulated that the Holy Spirit must be the feminine part of the Trinity and if humans were truly made in the image of God, "Male and Female created He them," then it was just as valid to call God "Mother" as it was to call him "Father." That didn't fly any farther at the dinner table than it did in my evangelical Christian school, but I thought I'd made a good argument.

Anyway, back to Rhonda. To think that she was interested in pagan religions at best, or mastering the dark arts of wicked witchery at worst...well, this was the type of situation us supernatural siblings needed to keep an eye on.

"Halloween, huh?" I said. "That'll make for an interesting holiday. Or, you could say no."

"And lose this one chance to win the wicked step-witch of the Southwest over when I have it? Oh, hell no."

"You know it's a losing game you're playing there."

"Guess we'll find out," my sister finished for me, and then turned away, mumbling, "At least she and I will have something in common to talk about for once."

I wondered at this, but I figured I'd find out later. Not my circus, not my show.

# −2−

So here it was Will's first MoonFall and I wasn't allowed to be there. I know, right? But Jackson said it wasn't good for Will's first change to be around me. Something about a lycanthrope's first moon fever usually caused the human personality to be subsumed and the only thing left was wolf, which meant they were going to have to run herd on Will anyway and didn't need little ol' me as a distraction.

Darla and Twyla were going out of town but I'd have Luken and Elka with me, or Elka at least. Since Luken was male, he might be included in the run.

Anyway, Elle actually offered to sit with me during my change. Of course if she did, she would most likely have the boys bring her La-Z-Boy and a widescreen down into the pool house basement. While we wouldn't be having any heart-to-hearts, she was good for ear scratches and tummy rubs, I figured.

Don't ask me how that works, my sister's partner and my wolf, but it did. I guess it was because she was a dog person. She seemed to find my lupine form easier to get along with than my human.

You know, I never thought about how it might be difficult seeing another version of her partner running around, but Elle was so shut down, I usually couldn't get a read on her at all. Best poker face on the planet; probably comes from her days as a trial lawyer. It must be unnerving to have Amber in her head all the time. I know it is for me.

It didn't end up mattering, though; I waved her offer to sit with me off, saying I had it handled. As expected, she just shrugged and went back to her ESPN.

Luken and Elka showed up after sunset. I'd made the change out on the hill behind the pool house and before the moon crested the horizon, and we'd settled in the basement cage. And no, I didn't lock us in. After a decade of changes I was pretty much in control of what I did when I was wolfed out, which also meant I was totally to blame when I slipped out on the sleeping ulv to go watch my boyfriend on his first turn. I'd fed them well, so they were sated and logy, which made it easy.

I know it was wrong to get near them, but I swore I'd stay downwind of the pack and it only took me about an hour to reach the top of Mt. Rettig and lay down on top of a rock overlooking the men as they stood in a circle in the meadow below me, above the crest of the falls. As they did, Paula, the river goddess who guarded Rettig Falls, sang a Stephen Schwartz number from Godspell, *Turn Back, Oh Man*, but I was a woman so didn't think it applied to me.

I know, I know. Talk about ignoring the obvious.

I don't care what some people say; I love looking at the human form naked in all its glory. Jackson Wolfe, tall and handsome, with dark hair and a natural pelt that matched his fur, reminded me of Hugh Jackman, only he wasn't as pretty and had more Native American in him. Don't know how well that translates, but that's what I've got.

Sullivan Kearney, on the other hand, is a much older silver fox, at least in human form. Sully made me think of Sam Elliott, compact form and lean muscles showing his years more than the rest of the brood as he changed.

Small and beefy Dex Watley – I have no one famous to compare – had cocoa-butter skin covered with black curly hair, reminding me of a Latin soccer player until he slipped into his camouflage covering as a wolf. Oh, and the Welsh brothers, Geoff and Neal Blalock, both smaller than Jackson, but built like beasts, with blue-black hair and fair skin, solid in flesh and fur.

And then there was Will, my Will Stenfield, younger than all of them and looking even more out of place with his pale English skin and farmer's tan. Since he'd taken the bite, he'd sprouted more fur, but he was still the least hairy of all of them. Even so, they were beautiful specimens, human and wolf alike – though I had yet to see Will slip the bonds of mundanity and show us his new nature.

They had told me that there might be some danger, it being his first turning, but Sully assured me that the pack magic should protect Will from the worst of it.

I sensed a presence nearby and felt the hand of my mother Anabelle, AKA Ghost Mom, settle on my head and scratch behind my ears. When I was lupine, I could pretty much feel her as if she was a live person, but when

I was human the most I got was the impression of being caressed by a Jean Nate-scented marshmallow.

"Not the wisest choice, sweetheart," she whispered in my ear, and I know she wasn't commenting on my metaphor.

I stifled a whine.

"I know you, and I know why, but I hope you're prepared for the consequences," she said as she faded out.

Well, nobody'd ever accused me of being wise, so I stayed where I was and held my breath.

The wolves below began to howl and my ears perked up; something seemed wrong. I could feel the tingle of pack magic like ants digging into my fur and I chewed my tongue, resisting the urge to howl with them.

Will seemed to be having trouble with the change, the smell of fear telling me he was resisting. *I knew this was going to happen,* I thought. I know visions and premonitions are Amber's territory, but at that moment I was glad I'd heeded my own doggie intuition. Will needed me.

I stood up to raise a howl, and all the voices of the pack died out as they turned to stare in my direction.

Will's eyes shifted first and he dropped to all fours. I don't normally pay attention to anyone's change but my own, but this was Will's first, and all I could think of was how incredibly scared he must be.

My heart went out to him and I whined as his body hit the dust and he rolled from fetal position into the most excruciating downward dog yoga pose I'd ever seen. Viscera poured off him as his skin split like cloth, the bloody bones of his spine cracked and reoriented themselves, waves of fur and new skin rushing to cover his form. He gave one last howl and gasp and collapsed.

The rest of the pack had shifted with him, and the wolves came forward to lick his pelt clean and welcome the new cub into their mix. Because that's what he was. His body may be adult wolf, but his lycanthrope mind was young and new.

He rose on unsteady legs and the pack gave him some room. Then, one by one, they all sat on their haunches and began to howl. And of course, silly me, I howled with them.

Then I didn't have time to think because Will the wolf joined the other males in a mad scramble up the hill toward me. Thank God experience and maturity beat newbie enthusiasm, 'cause the rest of the pack tore up the hill to surround me and place their bodies between Will and me.

At first, Will transmitted joy at seeing me, anger at being denied his mate, and then he vibrated with need. For what? I didn't know. Doggie Sex? Hunger and the lust to kill something while its blood ran down his throat? Or something entirely different?

Will's muzzle leaked fluid and his barks and howls threw slobber all over us. The rest of the pack stood silent, blocking his way shoulder to shoulder, until Will realized he was outmatched. He whined and dropped his head onto his forepaws, his haunches in the air, a typical translation of "play."

Jackson must have seen something I didn't, because he vocalized a great coughing growl-bark, which I interpreted as a command to *run*.

With a howl, Will launched himself into the air and cleared Dex's body, landing right behind me. And run I did. Thank God I was in better shape than Will, and faster. I was so not going to do the deed with Will his first time out, not until he gained some control and knew I was more than the wolf he currently thought me to be.

Natural wolves were clocked at about forty miles an hour at their fastest and have been known to travel 125 miles in a day. Lycanthropes and lupines? We're even faster.

So I ran until mountains became sun-dried meadows and became mountains again. I ran until Mt. Rettig blended with the Sierra foothills. I ran until the scent and sounds of pack were far behind me, though they never quite faded. I ran until I knew I'd better circle around or I'd never get back to Knightsbridge before sunup.

When I did, I had a lot to think about as I made my way home.

I had the pack at my door in the morning. Well, Amber's door. But JR let them in, and though he tried to text me on my cell, I was still passed out from the long night. They brought coffee with them, and God love 'em, they tried to be quiet sitting out on the back patio waiting, but the natural laughter and teasing that happened in pack mentality soon became too loud for my sister to ignore.

*Ashlee, get your ass out of bed and get the pack off my property!* Amber mind-screamed at me, sending me to the floor and scrambling for the shower.

"I'll get right on that, Roz," I mumbled.

Bleary-eyed, I threw on some denim short-shorts and a fire-engine red checkerboard bikini top and stumbled out of the pool house, not knowing how I was going to deal with the fallout of my transgression, but hoping that they would be more distracted by my assets than my disregard for pack law. The rest of the pack was dressed for the heat, so at least we matched.

Jackson looked at me and smirked, turning to Sully with a whisper. The rest of them eyed me like…well, like a pack of wolves. And then they all laughed.

I should have taken it better, but that got me mad, and I opened my mouth to blast them with a piece of my mind.

"Before you say something you'll regret, we're not laughing at you; well I guess in a way we are, but mostly we're laughing *with* you," Jackson said.

"Don't get me wrong, Ashlee." Sully sat me down and put a tall latte in my hand. "We love you, but what you did was incredibly stupid and could have ended in non-consensual canine copulation."

"That was *not* going to happen," I spat.

"Only because you happen to be lighter, faster and you have a lot more endurance than the rest of us," Dex said.

"Fine, I screwed up, but it all worked out. Happy now?"

"Come on. We can't stay mad at you, not only because you're so damn cute, but you're acting just like a teenager, testing your boundaries," Jackson said.

"Wow, now there's a compliment guaranteed to warm a girl's heart. And by the way, when I was a teenager I killed someone, so no, I don't think I'm acting like a teenager at all." Okay, I was kinda proving his point right now, I admit.

Jackson sighed. "We've all done stupid stuff. We're incredibly thankful that this didn't turn out different. We're glad you're okay. But what you did was not okay. We don't draw hard boundaries on pack law unless we have to. I'd like to assume that this is a one-time occurrence. Think about how Will would have felt…"

Will snapped, "Hey, now. Don't assume you all know what I think and feel. I knew what I was doing." Then underneath his breath he mumbled, "And you're not the boss of me."

Jackson gave Will a little snarl, but let the *faux pas* pass unremarked.

I sighed. We may not always like the feedback people give us, but relationships are often the best reflection of how we're doing. I guess the pack's the best mirror I've got to help make me a better lupine, not to mention human.

## 3

After I took a much-needed nap followed by a short crying jag on Will's shoulder as I licked my emotional wounds, we ended up rolling right into an impromptu barbecue with extended family, including the pack. They volunteered to buy groceries and Elle said she'd do the grilling right there on the deck. I liked this whole idea because it meant I could claim the leftovers when no one was looking.

Our former next-door neighbors Darcy and her daughter Tara came by. Amber had been BFFs with Darcy, and her brother Ollie and I had hit it off, staying best friends until he passed on. I never did see his ghost, which always made me sad; every girl should have at least one gay best friend, even if he's dead.

Elle stood at the grill making sure that everyone got their meat cooked to order, which for most of us was rare to blue, but there were a few who enjoyed their meat cooked well done. Yuck, ruins the flavor and, even worse, the texture if you ask me. If I had my way, every steak would be seared on both sides then allowed to run to the plate under its own power, dripping. You may think that's gross, but hey, were-girl here, you know.

I turned to Amber to ask if she needed anything as I made to remove the platter of meat waiting on the grill's sideboard, in order to fend off the rush of the salivating lycanthropes, when they both interrupted, "Don't touch the Hibachi!" But I think it was for two different reasons: Elle, because she was afraid that I was going to mess with her grill, and Amber, well, because she liked playing hostess and receiving accolades for her efforts and she hated for me to upstage her by serving the food. Which is fine, I mean, but I wish she would learn to chillax a bit.

I always thought Amber and I were like Mary and Martha. See, in this story, Jesus is visiting the sisters of Lazarus, you know, the guy that he resurrected. Well, there's this party going on; maybe it was to celebrate Lazarus' return. Anyway, Martha complains to Jesus that Mary isn't helping her out because her lazy sister is just sitting at the feet of Jesus, listening to him talk about spiritual things. Jesus turns to Martha and says, my paraphrase, "Martha, you're way too spun up about stuff that doesn't matter. Mary's hanging out with me, and I'm not going to tell her she's wrong."

So, good strokes to my ego, but underneath it all the takeaway message I got was this: relationships are what matter, not perfect hostessing, not the externals. Relationships with your higher power of choice, relationships with the people that the gods have brought into your life, family and friends. Like in Project Runway, people are here one day and gone the next, poof. Honor the time you have and share the love.

And yeah, I guess I judge my twin for being a doer and not a be-er, but it makes me sad sometimes. I think Amber misses out on the best things in life in her drive to make everything perfect.

But I digress.

As Amber brought the meat to the patio, the pack moved in and swarmed the table, passing over it like the dogs they were and leaving room for the second wave of food that Amber had waiting. I gotta give it to the girl; she sure can throw a party.

"Hey, honey, can you get me another beer when you get a chance?" Elle asked my sister as she was passing.

"Same flavor?" Amber replied, but as she always did, answered her own question. "Never mind, the usual."

Elle smiled at Amber as she returned to exercising her gift of hospitality and, in a rare moment of transparency I saw emotion in her eyes. I leaned over and put my arm around my sister-in-law and gave her a big bear, er, wolf hug. "Aww…."

"Go away Ashlee," Elle said, but she had a smile on her face, and I laughed as I let her be. Sometimes I enjoyed being a little shit-pot-stirrer.

I followed Amber inside to see if she needed any help, though she typically refused. I think she felt that I got in the way more than I assisted, but she was nowhere to be found until I heard her voice on the front porch.

Curious, I went to the door. She was just signing for a Fedex package and I smiled at the delivery guy as she sent him stumbling on his way with a bemused look. Hey, he was cute and I enjoyed the power of the twinship to confuse. Both of us, with the charm turned up, were pretty hard to resist.

Amber ripped open the package back at the kitchen counter, discarding the cardboard.

"Hearth Magic. Spells for Hosting and Hospitality," I read over her shoulder. "Since when are you learning witchcraft?"

She shrugged, turned to her shelf of cookbooks and added it to the library. "Just thought, since all this supernatural stuff is coming out of the woodwork I might as well educate myself."

"Hey, let me see that," I said and went to retrieve it.

"Don't break the spine."

I sighed. "I'm surprised you would need this at all; you already make magic in the kitchen."

"Research. Now that JR's in school I have a bit more time on my hands. Oh by the way, did you know that there's a lunar tetrad coming up?"

"What's a lunar tetrad?" Amber always enjoyed teaching me something I didn't know, and as long as it didn't carry any judgment about what I was required to do with the information, I didn't mind.

"Well, you know how a Blood Moon is a full lunar eclipse that turns red?"

"Yeah, not to mention it's the only time I can get pregnant with super-pups."

"Well, a lunar tetrad is four Blood Moons in a row. It's incredibly rare, happens oh…"

"Once in a blue moon," I finished for her, laughing.

Amber gave me a conciliatory smile. "And when a blue moon and a Blood Moon coincide, well that's one for the history books."

"What's a blue moon again?" I should know these things, but hey, that's what Google is for.

"A blue moon is the second full moon that appears in the same month. Normally there's only one full moon per calendar month."

"When's the next blue moon?"

"January, I think."

"And does it cross with the Blood Moon?" I asked.

"Yup. But what I'm worried about is this next Blood Moon as it crosses with a Witches' Moon."

"What, more moons? What's a Witches' Moon?"

"It's when a full moon is partially obscured by wispy clouds. It takes on a cool corona, like in ghost story movies."

"And when is that?" I asked her.

"September, this September."

"Coming up on Halloween, at least according to the stores selling candy. Well I'm not planning on getting knocked up anyway this year. Although if I did try, I suppose with a lunar tetrad I would have four chances to put a bun in the oven. And at least I won't have to deal with in vitro fertilization," I added, and then blanched as I saw pain cross my sister's face. It had cost Amber dearly in both money and suffering trying to get pregnant with John Robert.

"You can't mate over the lunar tetrad," Amber said.

"What do you mean I can't?"

"Not can't – really, *really* shouldn't, I mean. Especially not on the last Blood Moon of the Lunar Tetrad. This full moon is supposed to be a Witches' Moon. But combine that with a Blood Moon and you've got some very bad news."

"Like what kind of bad news?"

"I'm still doing research on that. Apparently, lycanthropologists are advising all moon-based shifters to forego mating over the lunar tetrad. They warn it will corrupt the natural order."

"Oh, please. I've heard this one before," I told her. "What's everyone afraid of, some wolfish antichrist?"

"This time I think you'd better listen, Ash. They're warning all weres to lock themselves up over the weekend."

"But why?"

"They're calling it Blood Moon Fever."

"Blood Moon Fever, eh? Where's Ted Nugent when you need him?" I made myself a mental note to take it up with the pack. "Well, at least it's not the apocalypse."

"I can send you all the research I've done."

"Since when are you doing research into full lunar eclipses, anyway?" Guess I should have been doing more research of my own. I'd gotten lazy, I know.

"Since my werewolf sister lives across the lawn from my six-year old son."

"Ouch."

"Don't ask if you don't want to know."

Then I heard Elle's voice from the backyard. "Hey Amber! Where's that beer?"

Sigh. Why does everything in my life have to be so complicated?

## 4

"Wanna go with us, Aunt Ash?" JR asked.

"Go where, honey?" I responded as I typed furiously on my latest freelance assignment: writing agenda copy for the Street Witches Convention. Amber got me the gig and I wasn't about to look a gift horse in the mouth. Maybe I could turn it into a real piece and sell it to a travel magazine for a Halloween issue.

"We're going to pick up the new dog from the pound."

"From the pound?" I turned to my sister who was shifting the contents of her day purse to the Michael Kors bag on her shoulder. "I thought you were only going with certified breeders," I said.

"Elle wanted a standard poodle and so started looking online at the shelters and rescue organizations. We got a call that there's a beautiful one in lockup right here in Knightsbridge," Amber replied.

"So, you haven't seen it yet," I said out of the side of my mouth as I chewed on a pencil.

*Ashlee that's disgusting,* she thought at me.

Thank God this Twin Bond 2.0 thing only worked one way. As far as I knew, no unauthorized mind reading. I used the frayed pencil to scratch my ear to see how far she would take it.

She ignored me. "No, but Elle has. And you know what she's like when she makes up her mind about something, she pretty much digs her heels in until she gets her way."

"Not like anyone else we know. So she wants a *poodle*? Why not get herself a labradoodle? Better personalities."

"I don't need a designer mutt," Elle said as she made a last check through the house. "Standard poodles have a long, dignified history as hunting dogs. You ought to appreciate that. And besides, you'll be impressed by this one."

"Now this, I've got to see," I said and grabbed my fanny pack and threw it around my waist. I know, it's ultra-nerd-retro, but it's a lifesaver if I ever have to force a change and still keep my stuff with me.

We stood in the main lobby of the Knightsbridge Animal Shelter waiting to be shown to the dog kennel. The place smelled of all manner of animal feces, hamsters, mangy cats and industrial strength disinfectant. I thought I was going to hack up a furball. Wait, that's cats, right? But that's how I felt.

Amber pointed me to the hand sanitizer. I'd already gotten rid of the pencil, but jeez.

"You know the last time we were here…" I began.

"Ugh. Don't remind me," Amber said as she flashed Sean Gottlieb's face at me across the twin bond. Jeanetta Macdonald's wasn't far behind.

Jeanetta was the skinwalker, a bruja, a Navajo-trained witch who tried to kill me last year. I suppose you could say her attempt at revenge was justified; I mean, I did accidentally kill her brother Shane during my first MoonFall after I turned sixteen. But she took the personal grudge too far by including Amber and Spanky in her machinations. She'd drugged us and dragged us up into the canyon, and when I awoke she was casting a spell to lock me into my lupine form once and for all.

Spanky broke her circle as she was causing me to shift and I took her down. She was remanded to the Central California Women's Facility at Chowchilla, where she still resided.

I shivered.

"Let's get this over with," Amber said as I watched the gooseflesh that was bothering me cross her own arms. It didn't seem like she minded the idea of another dog, just didn't like the process. After a bit of a wait – who thought it would be so busy at this time of the night? – they led us back toward the kennels.

Amber told us to go on as she stopped at the ladies room. Okay, she *really* didn't like the process. I bet she wasn't even going to go back there at all.

I hurried after Elle and JR, past yapping, barking, snapping, tired, old, and sometimes despondent canines that swept waves of emotion over me. I wasn't going to be able to stay here too long. It was too depressing. A dog needs to be free. Well, as free as they can be, domesticated and all. At least give the poor things nice back yards in which to spend the rest of their days.

A voice spoke into my head. *Hello? Hello? Is anybody there?* The voice was cultured, pitched like a low velvety growl with a lilt.

I looked around for the source, but all I saw were dogs. I'd heard that vampires could sometimes do the mind-speech trick, but nobody looked or smelled like bloodsuckers, at least not that I could see. I suppose there could be witchery going on. I readied myself for some sort of trouble.

Elle and JR had planted themselves in front of a large cage with a big snow-white poodle inside of it. I swear the thing came up to my hip. JR was *ooh*ing and *ahh*ing at the animal and had his hands inside the cage while the dog licked his fingers. Elle was already filling out paper-work with one of the workers. Signing things. No-nonsense, our Elle.

*You know it's quite rude to ignore a fellow when he's trying to make polite conversation.* The voice came at me once more and, as I looked around again trying to place its source, the poodle in the arms of my nephew was looking straight into my eyes.

*Oh shit,* I thought, and then, *whoever heard of a poodle shifter?* That was the next thing to come out of my head.

I heard the sound of a mirror cracking and felt a pain rip through my skull as I froze and stared at the apparently telepathic dog for at least thirty seconds. What the hell?

"Who are you talking to?" Amber asked, thankfully interrupting. Guess she managed to steel herself after all.

"No one." I shook the moths out of my head and looked at my sister again. She seemed...*off*. "What's wrong? You look like you've seen a ghost," I said, and then winced at the many-layered meanings in that one sentence.

"Not a ghost, Ashlee. Jeanetta Macdonald." She bit her lip and I could see the strain and frown lines struggle against the botox in her forehead.

"You had a vision?"

She nodded.

"In the bathroom? Of the pound?"

"Hey, I don't ask for them and I sure don't pick the place."

"So, what did you see?"

"I was fixing my face and tranced out for a moment. When I looked into my eyes, they weren't my eyes anymore. It was Jeanetta. Just her face. Floating in the bathroom mirror. But I swear she could see me, Ashlee. She got this incredibly gloating look on her face and she began to laugh. Next thing I knew, the mirror shattered.

"Oh, that's what that was."

"I beat a hasty retreat before anyone noticed the mess. Now, let's get the hell out of here."

That's my sister for you. Dodge the trouble and the awkwardness of actually reporting it. *Man, do I ever need a clove.*

*After what I just saw, I just might have one with you,* she twinned, grabbing my arm as we exited the building, leaving JR and Elle to finish up the adoption papers.

The dog's voice echoed in my head one last time.

*Till tomorrow, fair maidens!*

Great. More complications.

As we walked to the car I said, "So, what do you think that's about? Seeing Jeanetta in the mirror, I mean."

"I have no idea," Amber said. "But whatever it is, it can't be good if it's got her face attached to it."

"She's still in jail, right?"

"As far as I know."

"Maybe you should have Elle check for you. Have 'em put her in solitary or something."

"You can't just put people in solitary for nothing, Ashlee."

"I should have killed her when I had the chance."

"Ashlee, that's horrible!"

And she was right, it was. But three days out of the month I'm a total bitch. Guess it showed. Lost in thought, I took a long pull on the cinnamon-sweet tobacco, making a mental note to contact Jackson to ask about poodle shifters and what we should do if my sister brings one home from the pound. *Maybe I should call him right now*, I thought and grabbed for my phone. But before I pulled my contacts up, my sister put a hand on my arm.

Elle and JR came out of the building empty-handed.

"Where's the dog?" I asked.

"Doctor needs to give him his final shots and sign off on his release. We'll pick him up tomorrow," she promised my nephew, who was bouncing around like a jack-in-the-box.

*I'll call Jackson when I get home,* I promised myself and, of course, ended up forgetting as we girls got to drinking and telling stories over gin rummy after JR went to bed.

I woke up the next morning with Spanky barking on my bed, Elle standing like a silhouette in the pool house doorway with a mug of *café au lait* in her hand, and a poodle's snout in my crotch.

"Hey!"

*Hello again,* the dog thought at me as he stuck his head under my hand for a scratch.

"*Shift—*" I yelped, pulling my hand away and cradling my knees against me as Spanky barked at the poodle, who sat back on his haunches.

*There's no need for histrionics, young lady. I mean you no harm. Oh, and please don't tell them I'm not an ordinary canine,* the snowball white gangly prince of dogs continued in my head while I turned my "shifter" into "shit."

Elle was dressed for a hot day in tan cargo shorts and a periwinkle tee-shirt with an old school baseball cap on her head, Oakland A's variety. She smirked over her coffee. "I was going to introduce you to Siegfried, but it looks like you've already met."

"Gee, thanks." I scrambled for something to say as the poodle eyed me balefully and backed up.

Elle turned into the morning sunrise that was glaring its way through the door of the pool house and glinting off the fur of the poodle. I hung out the side window and watched her as she pulled the lawnmower out of the shed, and then a weed eater. "I checked with the warden. You'll be happy to know that Jeanetta's still safe and secure in the pokey. Oh, and Will's here." She headed around toward the front yard.

"Where's he at?" I yelled after her.

"Right here, sugar plum." Will rounded the corner and entered the pool house, growling at Siegfried, who gave him a wide berth as they passed each other in the doorway.

*Looks like time for a trim*, I thought as Elle checked the gas and the oil and then revved up the mower, heading out the back gate to the front yard. I went back to the futon I used for a sofa and sat cross-legged in its deep-blue pillowed depths. "Hi, hunky," I said.

Will threw a bag of donuts from Crave on the burnished table and mumbled something about going to the bathroom. See? Moody as Amber at that time of the month. It was pain enough when our cycles synched; I didn't think I could take much more of Will adding to the mix.

I got up to open the bag on the dining room table. Okay, with the studio layout of my new residence, I don't know if you could qualify it as a dining room. The main house may have been new when they bought it, but whoever did the original design on the pool house wanted a cross between a cabin and a cottage feel to it, as if they knew it would one day become an in-law unit.

Bet they never imagined my kind of in-law.

But I just loved the cathedral ceilings and the exposed beams. I had plans to use rope lighting for decoration, but hadn't gotten to it yet.

Will flushed the toilet, and then hopped onto the couch with me. Spanky jumped up behind him and he ruffled the miniature Schnauzer's silvery grey muff with both hands and then turned to make kissy noises to me.

"Dude, did you wash your hands?"

"Oh, hi, Amber. Didn't see you there."

I slapped him on the chest. "Bastard. You know it's me. Hands?"

"We're lycanthropes, Ash! A few microbes won't bother us, or Spanky for that matter. I mean, he's germier than either of us!"

I pointed. "Go. Wash. Hands."

He growled at me this time, but went to do it. "A standard poodle, huh?" he said as he returned.

"Guess so."

"Not the smartest dogs on the block."

*Yes, well this one obviously isn't from this block*, I thought. "Poodles aren't dumb. Just high-maintenance."

"Elle seems to like high-maintenance types."

"Good point."

"Um, Will…did you get a weird vibe from Siegfried?"

"No, should I?"

"I dunno, just…"

"Nothing beyond that of another mutt still trying to learn his place in the pecking order."

"Talking about him or you?"

Will punched my shoulder gently. "Funny. Why, what did Siegfried do?"

"Besides put his nose in my chonis?"

Will laughed. "That's my job."

I smacked him. With my backhand, not my lips. I guess all this smacking was the human version of wolf play-pawing.

"What? It's not like you've never had that happen before," he continued, and smacked me back.

I tried smacking him again, but he just tickled me into helplessness. Unfortunately, that caused a flashback to my pseudo-brother Whelan cruelly doing the same, which caused me to jerk a knee up into him. He was lucky I missed his jewels.

"Hey!" he exclaimed. Noticing the rage in my eyes, he said, "Hey. Ashlee, it's me. Just me. Nobody else here."

I began taking deep cleansing breaths to prevent a panic attack. Intellectually I knew what was going on, but my emotions weren't quite as savvy. "I need a clove," I said and grabbed one off the rustic coffee table along with my lighter and stepped out into the backyard clad only in my Scarlet Witch PJs. Hey it's my house too! Okay, it isn't, technically, but I live here.

At least I wasn't naked.

Spanky followed me as I moved to the right of the pool where I had a temporary weather-resistant patio set as a placeholder for when I could afford a real one. Amber had been bugging me to replace it, but I just didn't have the money. Priorities.

I sat on the forest-green plastic and lit up, pulling the ashtray toward me on the table. Spanky went to sniff out the competition, and soon he and Siegfried were frolicking in the yard. That was quick. I wouldn't have pegged those two as instant doggie BFFs.

Will followed me out and dangled the donuts and a carton of whole milk in my face. "So, what was that all about?"

I answered him in punctuated words. "Flashback. Tickling. Whelan." I took a drag on my clove and stared off into space, then shut my eyes as the bright sun made my eyes water.

He waited for me to gather my thoughts. I heard donut-munching sounds.

"When we were younger," I began, "eight or nine, I think. Pre-puberty, before the change and Amber's psychic powers started manifesting. One of the things that Whelan and Adam would do to torment us as kids was to tickle us until we cried 'uncle.' At first, we thought it was good clean fun. Amber would fold before I did, and when we did Adam would stop. But Whelan, he would go too far. As time went on, it took a sadistic turn. I eventually realized it wasn't about making us laugh anymore, if it ever was. It became about power. You know what it's like when somebody tickles you until you can't even breathe? Well, Whelan would do that. Adam even tried to stop him, but he was too little. Amber blacked out once."

Will held space for me as I decompressed the traumatic memory.

"So, one time I bit him."

Will looked appalled.

"Like I said, it was pre-turn and I didn't draw any blood, but Whelan slapped me in the face. This was when he was, like, fifteen and I was nine. Anyway, when the General found out he ordered Whelan to the garage and took his belt to him. We could hear him screaming bloody murder all through the house. I guess that's when we realized we were sleeping with the enemy under our own roof. Maybe more than one enemy. Dad put Whelan in the spare room off of the garage and though he never touched me again, Amber wasn't so lucky."

"That wasn't your fault."

"I should've known," I told him.

"How could you?"

"At the time I assumed whatever Amber knew, I would too because of the twin bond, but I guess she repressed that. I guess I can't help but think if things had gone different…if Whelan hadn't been so messed up, if Dad hadn't been such a dictator with his 'spare the rod, spoil the child' mentality, if he'd gotten him some professional help, maybe Whelan wouldn't be dead by now."

"Well, I for one am glad that the pervert is toast," Will said and bit into his donut.

I stared at him.

"What?" he asked, crumbs falling from his mouth.

"You're changing."

"I'm not changing."

"Yeah, you are."

"Oh yeah? How?"

"I don't know. You're more aggressive. Less compassionate. More matter-of-fact."

"More like a wolf?"

"A year ago you wouldn't have wanted Whelan dead, no matter what he'd done."

"A year ago you hadn't come home and we weren't in love with each other again, but I think I'd want anyone dead who hurt you." He reached out to cup my face. "Just because I'm not mourning the loss of your deadbeat brother who tried to kill you doesn't mean I've lost all my humanity."

That sounded so reasonable, but my internal fur stood up on end anyway, and it must have showed. He tried to take the clove out of my mouth, but I wrenched it away. "Get your own damn cigarette," I growled.

"Fine," he said, standing up to take off toward the side of the house, doing a running vault over the back fence. Thank God we don't have any neighbors on that side, just an open field between us and the woods. Damn, what was I going to do with that boy? He used to be able to put up with as much of my shit as I would dish out, but now he was getting so touchy.

"Ashlee!" came my sister's voice from the kitchen where she stood watching.

"I know, I know. Next time I'll tell him to use the friggin' gate." If there was even going to be a next time. His lack of empathy scared me and to be honest, I was afraid that sometimes my own lack of empathy was a slippery slope. But into what? I put out my clove and went back into the pool house where I sat cross-legged on the floor, trying to drown out Elle's mower with singer Deva Premal, meditating until the bad feelings went away.

Poodle shifter...now that was a problem, but not for now.

And speaking of problems, later on I caught Amber swirling her finger in a big jug of sun tea she was leaving out on the porch and mumbling something over and over, which was totally confusing, since her OCD about hygiene issues wouldn't normally allow her to even consider using anything but a fresh wooden spoon. When I listened more closely realized she was practicing a spell. Or maybe casting it?

*With this batch of unsweet tea*
*Steeped in solar harmony*
*Herbs from underneath the ground*
*Make my logic pure and sound*
*Water from the freshest spring*
*Air to bind the other three*
*Spirit brings tranquility*
*Namaste and Blessed Be*

So, it wouldn't bring any awards in the lyrics category, but what I was more curious about was what it was intended to accomplish.

"It isn't meant to accomplish anything specific," Amber responded to my unasked question. "I just have to talk to Elle later and need a little fortification."

"About what?"

"Stuff."

It was okay, she'd tell me soon enough. I just had to keep attacking her from different angles. "Where is she, anyway?"

"Homo Depot."

I laughed. "I thought it was Homie Depot."

"Manuel Labor, any time."

I had a flash of insight. "You're telling her about learning witchcraft."

"It's not really witchcraft, at least not in the Hollywood sense of the word. It's more wish-craft. A spell, like a prayer, is an offering, an invocation to the elements and to the Spirit behind it, from whom all blessings flow."

"I don't think your church would see it that way, considering they don't have much room for a feminine representation of God and have mostly ignored the presence of Wisdom Sophia in the Bible. At least the Catholics have Mary."

*An idolatrous idea to most fundamentalists,* Siegfried spoke into my mind.

*Damn you, dog!* I thought back at him.

*Looks can be deceiving. I am not a dog.* He lay down on the floor and let Spanky play leapfrog across his back.

"I only go to church because friends do," Amber said.

"I half-believe that, because you still half-believe."

She ignored me and plowed on. "As with any organization, you have to take the bad with the good sometimes. Doesn't mean I agree with everything."

"Well, unlike the Evangelicals and the Catholics, at least the dogs get along." *I am not about to tell Amber she has another shifter in the house,* I thought, and then slammed the twin bond shut.

She winced and narrowed her eyes at me. But hey, she was picking up my thoughts way too easily lately, and I needed to have some privacy in my internal monologue, er, dialogue, whatever, didn't I?

"Well, just be careful," I said.

"I know, I know. Power corrupts. I'm not stupid," she said.

And though I questioned this assertion, I let her have her justification as she went back into the house...for now.

The poodle caught my eye. *I'm not a shifter.*

"Then what are you?" I asked in a low whisper.

He whined as if the answer wasn't easy to explain.

I crossed my arms, pursed my lips and gave him my best Amber-style "I'm waiting" toe tap.

Siegfried sat on his haunches, and then hunkered down, laying his head over his front paws and looked up at me with puppy-dog eyes. *I'm a demon,* he said and my mouth dropped open even as my blood pressure hit the roof. *But, I'm a very bad demon, er, or at least not a very good one.*

"Wait, so you're telling me you're like a demon-possessed dog?"

"All witches' familiars are demons." Amber poked her head out the window. "Or daemons to be exact, as in d-a-e-m-o-n-s."

"You knew about this?" I looked at her incredulously.

"I suspected as much," she said as she came back out onto the patio with two glasses of iced tea that I eyed warily.

"And you're okay with this?" I asked.

"I have to be, though how I'm ever gonna break it to Elle that her dog is a daemon, I'll never know. The witch thing is going to be hard enough."

"Must be difficult for her, being the only muggle in the family. Can't you just take him back to wherever you got him?"

Siegfried looked at me wide-eyed and fearful.

"It doesn't work that way, Ashlee. A familiar finds the witch. A witch doesn't find the familiar."

"What, like when the student is ready, the teacher appears?" Or vice versa? Now I eyed my sister, the dog, and the iced tea with growing consternation.

"Something like that." She purposefully picked up her iced tea and drank it down, but I still wasn't going to take the Nestea plunge until she drank out of my glass as well and handed it back to me. "Besides, Elle's half in love with him already."

Siegfried gave me a tongue-lolling sloppy grin.

"Can you hear him like I can?" I asked her, taking a sip of the tea, and I swear I could feel the anxiety wash out of me.

"Not like you can," she sighed, "but when you've got the twin bond open, I catch echoes of his voice in your head and no, it doesn't work with Mom or I'd have let you off the hook by now."

*She has to find and cast the spell,* Siegfried said. *It's one of the first assignments for an apprentice witch. No shortcuts allowed.*

"I caught that," Amber said, and went inside to get her laptop.

"What spell?" I asked the dog.

*Familiar communication spell,* he replied.

"Isn't that, like, cheating? You just gave her a huge hint."

*I'm using what I have,* he said and placed his head on my leg. *Besides, having you for a sister, I'm thinking we need to fastrack, the b-, I mean, witch.*

I played with Siegfried's white curly mop that pouffed like Princess Leia's buns and scratched behind his ears until he started to lick my hand. I grabbed his muzzle and held it shut until he whined and when I let him go, he took my hand in his puppy sharp teeth, showing his unhappiness but not breaking the skin.

"Siegfried, no," Elle admonished him, coming out onto the porch with her own glass of iced tea and the sports section tucked under her arm. "Don't bite." She put the beverage down and gave him a whack on the nose with the paper.

*How humiliating,* his voice resounded in my head as he turned his attention to his "owner." *I was just marking you.*

*Ew,* I thought. *How about I hold you down while I pee on you? Now that's marking.*

"Refill?" Elle asked somewhere in the midst of this hard-to-follow three-way conversation.

*It's not that kind of marking. You know, you're pretty snarky for a girl human.*

"Refill?" Elle asked again and I shut Siegfried out so I could concentrate. And to be honest, I was feeling so good, I didn't want to say no, so I pushed my glass forward. "Shouldn't you be getting out of your PJs by now?" It didn't sound like a suggestion. This was the downside of an in-law old enough to be my mother. Well, if she'd had me at thirteen.

"Probably," I said, but that's as far as it got. My twin sister was a witch. Hope Dad never found out.

"You're what?" The sound of Elle's voice echoed through the main house from the garage where Elle and Amber had their workout equipment and held their "family" conversations.

I didn't mean to eavesdrop, but I didn't have anything in my refrigerator and well, the grocery store was four blocks away, and I didn't have a car and I was raiding Amber's fridge for…well, for something I didn't have.

Yeah, right. That's my story and I'm sticking to it.

"Are they at it again?" John Robert poked his head out of his bedroom.

"Hey sport. Yeah, but don't worry, I'm sure it's nothing." Hey, he had to live with my sister. I didn't. Poor kid. "Want a snack?"

"Lucky Charms," he said, bouncing onto the comfy davenport and turning on the television to drown out his parents while I made us snacks in the kitchen.

I could still hear them, though. Go lupines! Sometimes the hearing was a curse.

"You're the one who told me about the witches in the first place," my sister's voice echoed in my twitching ear.

"Yes, but I didn't expect you to become one!" Elle's voice resounded in the other one.

"And you're the one who wanted me to work the Street Witches Convention for the department over Halloween," Amber continued.

"That's because I think you're a shoe-in to take over Convention Services. If you want it."

"Of course I want it, eventually. Maybe when JR's a bit older."

"Why do you want to learn witchcraft, anyway?" Elle asked. "I thought we were doing fine with Joel Osteen and Joyce Meyer."

"I don't know, Elle. I guess it's because I need more than the power of positive thinking, something different from just a bearded old man in the sky who doles out miracles capriciously that tells me if things don't go my way there's something wrong with me."

"That's not how it really is and you know it."

"Well, that's how it feels sometimes."

"Just because that's how your father modeled the religion you grew up in, not because that's the way it is."

Interesting that Elle was supporting the party line, but she *was* older and more small-town traditional.

"Maybe it's because all the men in my life are screwed up."

"And most of the women. You're looking for something to blame. I didn't know you felt that impotent."

"I think disempowered is a more appropriate term." My sister sighed. "Anyway, so far it's just research. Besides, I'm probably just a hearth witch anyway."

"Have you done any of these spells?" Elle asked as I heard a rustling of pages and noticed the latest addition to Amber's cooking shelf was missing. I poured JR his cereal and added the disgusting fat-free milk she fed him. I mean, seriously, what was the point, if you're going fat free con lece; you might as well use the powdered stuff. Besides, kids need calories. I mean, look at me and Amber? We grew up on raw milk from a local dairy and we were both athletic and fit.

"Only a couple."

"Only a couple? Like which ones?"

I guess that's a lawyer thing to repeat the last words in a conversation, or what was coming from the witness stand in an interrogation.

"Just the tea of tranquility. It's supposed to be good for Ashlee's PTSD."

That bitch. So she *was* trying to medicate me after all.

Amber went on, "And the somnambulance snifter."

Elle choked. "You put a potion in my brandy?"

"You have been sleeping much more restfully lately. Better than taking Xanax."

"That's true, but not the point. You wouldn't put drugs in my food without permission, so why are potions okay?"

"Because they're made with love."

"It's not about love in this case; it's about respect, woman! No more dosing me without telling me."

"Or me either!" I yelled from the laundry room where I'd taken my eavesdropping to the next level.

I heard the garage door open amid mumbling, and the girls got into the Lexus and drove off.

"Sucks to be a grown-up, doesn't it?" JR said from behind me, though how he got the drop on me I'll never know.

"Yeah sport. Sometimes it indubitably does." I went back to the kitchen to fix us some more cereal. After all, I was still in my pajamas. Ah, the writer's life.

Five of us humans plus two dogs or doglike beings were sitting around in Amber and Elle's family room the next evening trying to use the TV to fill an awkward silence. Will had come over to bury the hatchet, or mend the fences, or whatever you want to call it. But I think he was just lonely since the pack had gotten called back to Montana for an emergency and he was left here without his boyfriends. I know, I know. I'm being snippy. But the mutt was working my last nerve.

I'd been ruminating on what to call the daemon dog, because Siegfried was an awkward mouthful, which constantly reminded me of those lion tamers in Vegas, and had me wondering whether or not they were real lions and tigers in their act or if maybe there were shifters, and if the reason nobody talked about Siegfried's injuries from the animal attack is because secretly they were shifters bent on revenge, when JR rescued me from my internal story-making.

"I'm bored." JR said, voicing what most of us were thinking as we stared at whatever mindless entertainment was being offered on the boob tube. Yes, I did call it that, even though there aren't as many boobs on American television as there are in other countries, and there actually are no more tubes in televisions, I think. Or maybe the boobs were the ones watching.

Will turned to me and said, "Let's go cruising."

Before I had a chance to say anything in response, JR crowed, "Yeah! Woohoo! We're going cruising! American Graffiti style!" and went to put on his shoes. He'd been raised on that movie, as – did I tell you this before? – George Lucas had grown up in nearby Modesto and the movie was set there, and its success had given him enough juice to have Star Wars made, another of JR's favorites, of course.

"What a great idea!" Amber turned to Elle. "We should all go. We can take the SUV."

Elle narrowed her eyes at Amber.

"Hey, I think if I'm going to be a part of the Street Witches, I should probably see up close what they're doing," Amber continued.

"I suppose." Elle followed Amber to the bedroom to change from slippers to sneakers. I grabbed the jug of sun tea from the porch and went back to the pool house to stock up on cloves and fill a water bottle with Ashlee's Long Island Tea of Tranquility. Hey, if I was going to revisit my glory days – or the sins of my past – I was at least going to be fortified with something better than Amber's potion, California's open container laws be damned.

*I call shotgun!* Siegfried dashed for the garage as we headed for the vehicle. I guess the dogs were coming on this excursion as well.

John Robert sat between his moms in the front seat and laughed as we drove down Olive to the Foster's Freeze next to the White Rabbit, a popular bruncheon spot for the aspiring magick crowd, landmarking the beginning of Main Street, Knightsbridge, California, USA.

At the edge of the street, a group of women, children and a few men, all dressed in all shades of yellow, poured out of a large lemon-colored pup tent and ran around. Some waved saffron streamers on sticks; others twirled flags, set off rainbow blooming flowers or fought over a couple of blue-and-canary lawn chairs. They sold drinks from a Knightsbridge Trojans cooler and sported a big banner that announced them as Station #1 of the Street Witches, Eastside Daughters of the Eternal, or SWEDEs for short. That seemed appropriate, given the many Scandinavians who'd settled the town so long ago.

We rolled up beside them on the side of the street and Elle rolled down the window.

"Hey Bea," she said, and the whole car echoed as a half-familiar woman stuck her head in and gave us a brilliant smile.

"Hello, ladies and gentlemen." She gave Will a nod and settled her warm sunny disposition onto my nephew. "Well, what have we here? I've never seen you around here before and I know everybody."

"It's just me, Aunt Bea," John Robert responded, and dawned on me that we were looking at JR's Sunday School teacher, Beatrix Soderstrom. The oddity of a witch holding that job would hit me later.

"Well, this is a pleasant surprise. Inaugural run, is it?" she asked him.

"First time for everything." Amber smiled.

"Well, Team Gordon-Scott," she admonished with a wag of her finger, "obey all street signs, keep it moving, and Chinese fire drills only at stop lights with a Street Witches station on the corner."

"What's a Chinese fire drill?" JR asked.

"You'll see!" we all answered together, laughing. Oh, this was going to be fun.

"What's a Chinese fire drill? What's a Chinese fire drill?"

I swear the kid did not let up until we hit Station #2, Street Witches Northside Brothers of the Eternal, or SWiNBEs, as they said it. Yes, the acronym was a bit more forced. This station held mostly men and their children dressed in green, with kids holding glow sticks and waving around emerald sparklers.

We rolled up to the red light. Amber and I looked at each other from between the seats and screamed, "CHINESE FIRE DRILL!"

The universe seemed to slow around us, the people thronging downtown stopped to watch as colored lights from above spotlit the car. We all clambered out of the vehicle and made one revolution of the SUV before climbing back in and starting the car again just as the light turned green. It always happened that way, and everyone clapped and laughed as we drove on.

"Oh my gosh. I was so afraid we weren't going to make it," Elle deadpanned as JR hopped up and down on the seat.

"Let's do it again! Let's do it again!"

And though I know it might be fun for him, I realized that I'd begun feeling claustrophobic. "Hey Elle, can you pull over at the next street witches station. I think I'd like to walk for a while."

"Me too," Will said, which was fine.

She stopped at Street Witches Station #3, Southside Sons of the Eternal, or SWiSSE, and let Will and me out among the crowd gathered there. These men were a bit more somber; maybe it was the color red that seemed to portend something disastrous. I think the colors had something to do with the cardinal directions, but I couldn't remember what red stood for. I'd ask Amber later.

Will walked beside me and as natural as breathing slipped his hand into mine. "Quarter for your thoughts?" he asked.

I snorted. "A quarter?"

He shrugged. "Inflation."

"What happened to a nickel or a dime?"

"What can you get for a nickel or a dime anymore?"

"You can get nickeled-and-dimed."

"Or get a dime dropped on you."

"By Professor Plum in the dime store with the nickel-plated revolver."

"I haven't a clue what you're talking about."

"Exactly."

"Wierdo."

"Maniac."

"Lunatic."

"Luna, moon. Ooo, that's actually spot-on. So I was thinking about the pups," I began.

Will interrupted. He was doing that a lot more than he used to and it was annoying. "Me too."

"I think we should –" I said.

"I think we should –" he said simultaneously

…And I said, "wait," while he said, "do it soon, do it now!"

Hoo, boy.

"Will, you just turned. You've only experienced one MoonFall and frankly I think we need a little more time together before we become puppy parents."

"Okay, I get that. But it's only going to affect you while you're turned, right?"

"I don't know that. Maybe. Probably. That's what I'm told. Worst-case scenario puts me in a perpetual state of PMS. But I'm a little more concerned about *your* behavior lately."

"Yeah, I've been a *gen-u-wine moody bastard*," Will said in a Sam Elliot drawl, mimicking Sully, who obviously must have called him that at one time or another.

"Glad we agree on something." I tried to pull away but he snuggled up closer to me.

"Grr," I growled, only half annoyed.

"Grr," he growled right back as we walked, shoulders pressed together.

"Hey Ashlee! Lookin' good!" Greg Anderson, an old school chum, yelled at me from his tricked-out convertible roadster with the top down. The girl in the front seat next to him waved.

I laughed. "Hey Kira! Can you please keep a leash on your dad? I'm already taken, thanks!"

Will stood stock still in his tracks, nostrils flaring.

"WILL!" I had to step in front of him as his blue eyes began to glow – yes, literally glow – with an amber corona around the iris. "Will," I began again, softer this time, hugging him to make sure he didn't move. "Honey. Greg is just an old friend from high school. He's married. We never even dated. You remember him, don't you?"

"Argh," he answered. "Sorry. I just. I've never thought about myself as the jealous type. I mean, I always knew a part of me was an animal, but…"

"But now that means more than you ever bargained for?"

"Guess so," he said. "It scares me. It's like times ten."

I stared up at him, my chin pointed at his, and waited. People flowed around, ignoring us. Plenty of lovers on the streets, the night and the lights relaxing the usual small-town standards, ice cream cones or pretzels or churros or drinks in their hands. At moments like these, Main Street in Knightsbridge seemed like Disneyland, warm and magical.

Will said, "You know my dad had a temper. He only snapped once, but it was pretty nasty. Went on a bender. Said some horrible things to my mom and me. Came to us the next day weeping at our feet begging for our forgiveness. I don't know which was worse, his anger or his shame."

"You're not him."

"We're all products of our parents and our upbringing, Ash. For better or for worse. I know it's cliché, but I don't know if we actually make any choices in our lives or if it's just circumstances making us dance like puppets on strings."

"The fact that you're struggling with this shows *we* choose."

"You didn't choose to be a…" He lowered his voice and pulled me over to an unoccupied bench, out of the way of the foot traffic. "You know."

"But I do choose what to do with it," I replied, stroking his cheek. "You're having the equivalent of your first period, hon. I know it ain't much fun, but it will settle down as you get used to it. Remember, your response is your responsibility. Control your emotions or your emotions will control you."

"You're one to talk."

I sighed. "Oh, I know. I can be bad sometimes, but I'm not six-two and well known in town. And my livelihood doesn't depend on *not* being arrested for assault."

"I dunno. It's hard to be a travel writer from jail. Okay, I get it." He took my hand and brought it down. "But about the pups…"

"I think we need to wait a while," I said. I wanted to seem like the perfectly reasonable girlfriend when I know I'm not, but I also wasn't ready to be a mommy, dog or human. Or hybrid, either. I wondered what would happen if two lycanthropes in wolf-man form mated. Have to ask Jackson about that one sometime.

"Yeah, I guess you're right," Will said as we neared Station #4, Street Witches Westside Sisters of the Eternal, dressed appropriately all in blue. These abbreviated their piece or sect or chapter as SWWaSE, which for no particular reason made me thing of Swayze in Ghost.

What's weird was, standing right next to them were Elle, Amber, JR and Ghost Mom. I guess they had pulled over somewhere and got out. Behind the crowd was a man dressed like a Mormon missionary, on a podium with a bullhorn.

The parking lot of Youngdale's was the official terminating point of Main Street before it made a 45-degree angle due west and became tree-lined West Main, making a beeline toward the California coast a good two hours away. It was also a gathering place for those who enjoyed walking the downtown stretch rather than driving it, and it included many families.

I guess recently it had also become a staging point for the evangelists who believed it was their job to save the world, one convert at a time, God love them. Don't get me wrong, I'd prayed the prayer, too many times probably. I had my fire insurance – once saved always saved, after all – but hellfire and brimstone? This was new for Knightsbridge.

"Repent, for the End of Days is at hand! Beware the prophecy of the Blood Moon which forecasts the coming of the apocalypse," he bellowed. "Don't waste your life cruising Main Street! Turn to God, not these spawns of Satan claiming to protect you as they usher you up and down the main street of perdition! Wide is the road that leads to destruction and narrow the gate that leads to everlasting life!"

I wasn't quite sure how he connected cruising with the apocalypse, and if he really knew his Bible he might have run across "by their fruits shall ye know them." And I'm pretty sure there's no mention of a Blood Moon anywhere in Holy Scripture. I googled the phrase and "Bible" just to be sure.

Nope, no Blood Moon, not even in the Book of Revelation, though at least once the moon turns red as blood.

Ya think?

Naw.

Still, his words seemed to resonate. As I pondered the incoherent rambling of the street preacher and the excess of Polo cologne covering his sweaty skin, I decided I'd better find out more about this Blood Moon prophecy. Maybe he'd tapped into something. I'm pretty sure Aleister Crowley had said, "The spiritual is like a box of chocolates. You never know what you're gonna get." Or something like that.

Meanwhile, Amber looked like she was having a heated argument with Elle, who was holding on to her elbow keeping her from tackling the preacher. The last thing we need here in Knightsbridge is a fanatic calling us all sinners and scaring away the tourists.

I think everyone knows deep down they are sinners, after all. I mean, who hasn't done something wrong, even mean and nasty? But it was kind of like "everybody poops." We don't need to have the details thrust in our faces when we're trying to have a nice evening out. There's a time and place for a life-changing epiphany of guilt, usually right after hitting rock bottom and right before deciding to enter a twelve-step program, but this wasn't it.

I'm only partway being facetious on that one. I know there are those who believe that the world is going to hell in a hand-basket, but I choose to believe that the Eternal Divine still has His and Her hand on humanity, hoping we'll one day sort ourselves out, with a little help from above, I suppose.

Anyway, Ghost Mom had her insubstantial arms around JR, who in turn had his hands full with Spanky, who was barking like mad at the street preacher. He was also juggling the pull of Siegfried's leash around his wrist, though how he ended up with both dogs, I don't know. Ghost Mom was losing the fight to help, and JR got dragged away from the Street Witches' encampment to stand in front of the missionary.

Will and I hurried to cut him off at the pass, but it was too late. The street preacher stopped speaking to look at the child, nonplussed. Okay, not such a bad thing, I guess. "This is no place for good young men," he said, wiping his forehead. He was *so* not dressed for an evening in the high eighties.

"My dog doesn't like you," JR said with perfect, nonjudgmental sincerity, like he was merely conveying indisputable fact.

Siegfried agreed by baring his teeth at the sweaty man.

"My other dog doesn't seem to like you either," he went on.

"I'm more of a cat person," the street preacher said and grinned. He actually had a little bit of charm if you could get past the cologne. But cats? Hell, no.

So, maybe I'm prejudiced, but I don't trust cat people. Never had, never will. Anyone who could put up with the manipulative, coy, fickle personalities that typically come with cats makes my inner wolf sit up and take notice. Unless it was a lion or a tiger, I think she thought that the word cat meant *prey*. I, me the human, just thought they were nuisances. Maybe you know more than I do, but if cats are an acquired taste, then I was sensory-deficient in that area. Although they might taste good, I mused.

*And we don't play with our food*, Siegfried commented. *Most of the time.* And then he bit the man. Okay, actually he merely closed his mouth gently on the man's hand as he had with mine. It wasn't Siegfried's fault the guy yanked it out of the poodle's jaws, catching a ring on the dog's teeth and drawing blood.

"Siegfried, No!" Elle grabbed Siegfried's collar and pulled him away.

*Mmm, tasty,* Siegfried said in my head.

"Oh my gosh, sir. Are you hurt?" Amber asked, putting on her most polite customer-service solicitousness and hiding any of her usual intolerance for children and fools.

Oh, yeah, that was me. Amber is much better at soothing ruffled feathers than I. Me, I was enjoying the smell of fresh blood in the air. But Will was growling, and that wasn't good. I dug my nails in his arm and pulled him away from the crowd and into an alleyway.

"I'm losing it, Ash," he said, his eyes glazing over with bloodlust.

"Just breathe, babe. Take long, deep breaths."

"I don't wanna take deep long breaths. I wanna take my claws and –"

I cut him off there. "And what? Rip the guy limb from limb?" I raised my voice and got into his face, my alpha against his whatever. I knew it was a power play and normally I wouldn't do it, but somebody was going to have to get this under control and since the pack wasn't here, I guess it was going to have to be me. "Because I've done that, Will. And it's not pretty!"

That got through to him, I guess, enough so he calmed down. His eyes turned human again and he laughed ruefully. "Okay. I got it."

And though I wanted to be mad at him, I just couldn't. You've got to have a morbid sense of humor as a werewolf, otherwise you'd be crying all the time. So, to take all the sting out, I kissed him.

We turned back to see how the scene was playing out, and I noticed Con Shelby, in his usual suit, hat and walking stick, stepping up behind the agitated street preacher. Hey, I didn't really blame him for being agitated, what with a big white daemon dog appearing to bite him.

Anyway, I got that itchy feeling in my sinuses just as Shelby tried some kind of fang magic on the guy. I said "tried" because whatever it was, he botched it miserably, or at least it failed.

Worse than failed, it seemed to backfire. The man spun around and pointed with his Bible like a gun, yelling, "I see you, Spawn of Satan! I feel your presence! Get thee back to thy grave and stay there!"

I'd thought this guy was all talk, but when Shelby reeled back and had to be caught by several members of the watching crowd, I knew something more was going on. Whatever mojo he had, it was enough to take a vampire off guard.

Shelby staggered to his feet and straightened his lapels, giving the man a shrewd, though not particularly angry, glare. "I'm no more familiar with the grave than you, Mister Willoughby, and I'll trouble you to cease your assaults upon my person."

I wondered how Shelby knew his name. Maybe magic, maybe he'd just seen the man around before.

Willoughby said, "So it is always with the evil ones, attacking first and then claiming offense when they are defeated by righteousness."

The guy had a point. Con Shelby had tried his magic first, and I was enjoying him getting the best of the vampire, really. Jackson insisted Shelby was a necessary evil – okay, he said necessary *part* – of the supernatural order, but I still didn't like him. Maybe a bit of discomfiture and comeuppance would teach the fang some humility, which was something he could dearly use. Even a lion could get gored by a wildebeest now and then.

Shelby raised his voice. "Let he who has never sinned cast the first stone."

"I cast only the second stone. Get thee behind me, Satan."

The crowd was growing. If Shelby wanted to de-escalate, he was going about it the wrong way. He seemed to realize that, so he saved what face he could by tipping his hat, turning on his heel and striding off.

I saw Elle talking on her cell phone, and it wasn't more than a minute before two bicycle cops showed up and got Willoughby to leave, first on the basis that he was on private property and the First Amendment didn't apply, and secondly that he was creating a public nuisance. It's nice to be part of the government at times like these, but the whole thing still made me uncomfortable. People should have a right to protest, even if we didn't like what they said. But it was out of my hands. Whatever the cops told him, he eventually packed up and left.

With the crowd dispersing, Will started kissing me again, and okay, I kissed back. It looked like it was going to be an athletic night for both of us. That was one thing about Will's new status that I had to adjust to – boundless energy in bed. And I mean boundless. Good thing I was a were-girl, or I'd never have been able to keep up.

A cough brought us back to ourselves as we realized that the SUV had pulled up beside us, and Elle and JR were grinning out the window. Amber just looked annoyed. But I guess that's what happens when you're in a high-visibility position in the local government. No PDA in front of the unwashed masses.

"So, what did you think of cruising Main Street?" Elle asked JR as we buckled up and headed for home.

"I think it's cool. It's just like American Graffiti, only not in ancient times," JR pronounced with the pompous gravity only a child can muster, to which the whole car erupted in laughter.

From the mouths of babes, I thought, and though I was still a bit miffed at Will's lack of control, I scooted into his arms and wrapped myself in his newfound passion, trying not to worry about what the future would hold.

Though I did tell myself to have a conversation with the Con-man later.

# –6–

"Hey, I've enchanted this new tea tree salt scrub for your feet, and get this: the key ingredients include seaweed and microscopic fish scales. Wanna try it?" Amber asked, a little bit too over-eager to employ me as a guinea pig for her budding magical skills. "I used it myself."

I have to admit her feet looked perfect, and I do have the worst calluses that build up on my paws and I didn't have the money for a weekly pedicure right now, so hell, spell away. "Yeah, sure, why not. Oh and how are you doing with that familiar communication spell? Ziggy's bugging the crap out of me because you won't talk to him."

"His name's not Ziggy, and I won't talk to him because he's supposed to be a gosh-darned poodle. And I'm afraid if I start hearing him in my head I won't know how to block it, and won't that be kinda creepy hearing his voice all the time, just another one to add to the peanut gallery, and before you know it I'll be looking like a crazy person talking to my dog. Oh, and then I'll have to tell Elle, and she really likes that dog, but I think this one might tip her right over the edge."

Amber's verbal vomit ran on and on, and I just gave her space and let her rant. Hey, it was the least I could do.

Especially since a part of me wanted to dance around pointing fingers. I already told her that the sooner she tells Elle about Ziggy the better. I'd decided that Ziggy was a much better name for the dog, as it didn't force me to constantly face my lack of being able to get my mouth around another language. Better she deal with reality as it is than get caught in a big fat lie when the illusion shatters. I thought she'd learned that with Mervin, but hey, we all do stupid things.

Who am I to judge, right? I had my own sins to atone for and I was sure I'd be eating my words soon enough. Make a pronouncement about who you are and the universe gives you the opportunity to show what you're made of.

"Not to mention that I keep having these recurring nightmares where everywhere I turn I see Jeanetta Macdonald staring back at me."

"What, like that Denzel Washington movie where he was up against that demon who kept jumping from person to person?"

"Exactly."

"Have you looked in that cookbook for a potion against nightmares?" I asked.

"Like that's not the first place I tried. I may have to break down and go to Bell, Book and Candle. Oh, and if anybody sees me and asks, I'm going to pretend to be you."

Bell, Book and Candle was a mystical shop that stocked herbs, crystals, incense and a whole slew of books on obscure religions. I'd tried to go in a few times, but between magick allergies and the myriad bouquet of essential oils that made my eyes water, I'd had to escape the overstimulation of my senses before it left me hacking up a fur ball on the manicured lawn. Like many of the downtown shops in Knightsbridge, it was once somebody's home, from the time when people didn't mind living their whole lives on the main thoroughfare. Privacy wasn't such an issue back then, I guess, and people used to sit on their front porches and socialize.

I kind of missed that. Sometimes I sit outside on Amber's porch and nobody comes up to talk to me. Best I get is a wave. Guess that's what the McMansion set does.

Or it could be my smoking. Used to be that smoking provided a bonding moment among an obscure set of people with a similar habit. Unless you count the stoners, now it tends to isolate rather than attract. Sigh. I miss the Bay Area vibe, but Amber would never put up with a bunch of my friends from Berkeley camping out on her front lawn, no matter how big it is.

"Why am I going to BBC again? We ought to keep our stories straight."

"I don't know. I'll make something up."

"Christ, Amber. I have enough of my own sins to atone for; don't make me responsible for yours."

And my twin sister did it. That's right, she snorted. Wish I could have captured it on video.

Anyway, we sat down on the edge of her garden tub and Amber slathered this fishy-herbal-flowery smelling stuff on my feet. She bent over with a pumice stone doing something I normally wouldn't think to do myself, and I realized that

this was what family was all about. The simple things –
moments together full of resonance. Where even the tiniest
deed like a foot rub can make me tear up, or maybe that was
the fish scales. Or the enchantment.

Still, when the pack came back I was deliriously happy.
It appeared that not only could Siegfried communicate
with me, but the lycanthropes understood him as well. I
had no idea why. I gathered that neither magic nor magick
was always logical.

So when Amber decided to hold an afternoon tea and
registration-packet-stuffing party for the Street Witches,
my offer to help was in hopes that I could figure out how
to move Amber forward with her familiar communication
spell, and also see if there was a way to get Ziggy out of
my head. After all, daemon though he might be, there was
something about him that didn't always scream dog. And
that was just freaky.

Amber decided on a cream silk blouse and pressed
linen trousers for the event, and for once let me raid her
closet. I decided on a summer-slipping-to-fall-toned lapel
vest over a coral tube top and white cotton culottes with
matching boat shoes. The Street Witches wore everything
from Stevie Nicks black flowing numbers to peasant skirts
and pirate shirts to spandex, denim, daisy dukes and straw
cowboy hats.

Now, even though we saw men as part of the Street
Witches on Main Street, it soon became apparent that this
gathering was entirely of females, or at least it appeared so.
I wasn't about to check everyone for Adam's apples.

Amber didn't seem to have much use for men in her everyday life.

Anyway, all the scents and excess magic dust swirling off of the Street Witches made my normally sensitive nose unreliable. Even Amber had a moment of distress and had to go retreat to the bedroom for her inhaler, while I did the unthinkable and opened all of the windows in the house and I ran the air conditioning at the same time. But hey, asthma and allergy attacks are no fun.

When the attending witches realized what was happening, they decided that it would be best if they began the gathering by calling the corners. Said it would calm the mystical energies in the atmosphere that tended to get stirred up when a lot of witches gathered in one place. They did this by calling us into a circle – okay, it was more of an oval – and spinning a beer bottle. Elle had left enough of those in the recycling bin and it turned out to be quite effective.

The presiding witch, who asked us to call her Sister Lena, strode into the circle wearing an emerald bustier and corset barely covering her massive and impressive torso, and a rich burgundy tea-length skirt obscuring black combat boots. Holding her gnarled Bo-Peep staff with shining threads cobwebbing a ruby crystal, she spun around in an incantation.

"Namaste and Blessed Be," she said, and we all answered.

"The first thing we do at the start of every gathering is we take care of logistics. Do we have needs, concerns, prayers or offerings to the Goddess this afternoon?" At which point, hands were raised, support was requested and, surprisingly, it wasn't much different from a praise service crossed with a prayer meeting.

"With these in mind," Sister Lena said when the preliminaries were complete, "let us sing."

As one they raised their voices and began chanting songs I later found out were called things like "Cauldron of Changes," "Earth, Air, Fire, Water" and "Sisters of the Moon." I became caught up in it. There weren't many places in Christendom where the Divine Feminine was extolled and it did my heart good to remember that I was a chip off the sacred block.

When the last notes of song dissipated, Sister Lena spoke, "Let us call the corners," and with her staff she spun the bottle.

"Sister Bertrille," she said, and I fought back a snort. Sister Bertrille was the name of the Flying Nun. Obviously Bertrille's mother had a sense of humor, or maybe she just liked the classic TV show. People used to tell Amber and me that we looked a bit like Sally Field, especially when we were younger; I sure hoped we aged as well.

"Come Element of the East, we call you. Arise, oh spirit of the East, whose color is yellow like that of the rising sun and the sunflowers that open to meet the day. Come place of new beginnings, refresh us as we gather. Welcome East."

"Welcome East," we all intoned.

The bottle spun again. Another, Sister Nayala, stepped forward.

It seemed witches really enjoyed emphasizing their sisterhood. Girl power!

"Come Spirit of the North. Whose color rides in shades of green. Whose bounty speaks of death and rebirth, resurrect our hearts and minds. Let us maximize our time and potential as we gather. Welcome North."

"Welcome North," we repeated. I looked over at my sister and I had to stop and take a breath. She was usually so high-strung, but tonight, she seemed at peace. And we hadn't even drunk the kool-aid. I mean, the tea of tranquility.

The bottle spun again and surprising, it stopped aimed toward me. Now, I wasn't a witch, but I *have* seen the movie *The Craft* a few times, and so I stepped into the circle and went with it. I *am* a writer after all. Hell, I eat metaphors for breakfast.

"Come Guardians of the Watchtowers of the West, we invoke you. Come blue tinged waters and deep azure skies, let the tempest be stilled and our emotions run deep under ebony stars. Come West."

*Ebony stars would be dark, lupa,* Ziggy thought at me from the garage. He must have pretty good hearing. Of course he did! He was a dog, or at least inhabited the body of one.

*Everyone's a critic,* I thought back at him and returned my attention to the matters at hand.

"Come West," the sisterhood of witches repeated and with shining eyes I stepped back into my space in the circle.

My own sister shot daggers at me and I realized I might have made a serious error in judgment. Not my circle. Not my show. And I just stole it. But come on! What was I supposed to do, refuse? If she didn't want me involved, why invite me?

That was sisterhood for you too, the bad with the good.

The bottle spun again and another sister claimed the stage and we welcomed the south, with its fiery reds and passionate fire, amazon warriors and keepers of the hearth. But all I could see was the fury in my sister's eyes. Nothing like stealing your sister's thunder in her own house. I winced and saw a storm cloud headed my way.

After the circle, Amber laid out piles of paperwork with the Street Witches logo on everything to be stuffed into the registration packets. The witches began passing out iced teas to each other, along with snack plates of cucumber sandwiches and *petit fours.*

*Don't muzzle the ox while she is threshing,* I thought, then I took Sister Bertrille aside – hey I liked her name and at least she wasn't wearing the wimple – and began quizzing her about familiars. Okay, well, I pretty much dumped the load onto her shoulders and begged for her help.

"Can you please, please, please help my sister with the familiar communication spell, because I need to get that damn dog out of my head and right now, I'm the only one he's talking to!"

Sister Bertrille made the appropriate sympathy sounds, then told me that she would see what she could do. Before I knew it she pulled Sister Lena aside and whispered in her ear. A short while into the small talk and stuffing, Sister Lena turned to Amber and said, "I hear you have a standard poodle as a familiar. Siegfried, is it? Where is he?"

"Oh, we put him and Spanky – that's our miniature schnauzer – in the garage for the afternoon. They are so rambunctious and the last thing I need is to have these piles rearranged for us by the animals."

"Oh please, can we see him?" Sister Nayala asked, and a few of the other witches chimed in.

"We've only heard of a few dog familiars, and a standard poodle is definitely a first for us," Lena added.

Guess we were having show and tell. It was about time.

Amber squinted her eyes at me over her reading glasses and then went to the garage door. "Spanky, no," she said. "Siegfried, come." And I heard the dog-thing trot over and follow her into the open space that flowed from the kitchen into the informal dining and family room. Amber kept her petite hand on his collar.

"What a beautiful specimen," Sister Lena commented and the rest of the witches *ooh*ed and *ahh*ed.

"He doesn't behave very well, at least not yet. We just got him from the pound," Amber said. "Siegfried, sit."

He did.

Sister Lena raised her hand and the standard white poodle trotted over to her and sat at her feet. Without a treat. She looked into his eyes and I could feel the communication going on, but for once I was not privy to its contents, thank God. Give me my own head space for a bit.

Lena looked at Amber and said quietly, "He says you haven't done the familiar communication spell."

"Not yet." Amber looked away and it suddenly dawned on me: she was scared to try. "I'm not scared," she answered my unspoken comment. "I just. I guess, I mean, it feels like if I do this, then…"

"There's no going back," I finished for her.

"Yeah," she said, and then shut down the bond.

"And you're afraid of…?" Sister Lena said.

"What if someone finds out? What will I ever say?"

"Whose business is it anyway?" I asked. "As long as you fly under the radar."

"Yes, but what about Rhonda?" she blurted.

"Oh." I'd forgotten about that. Our stepmom has a terrible history as a gossip. For a while there, after my Dad and she got married, it seemed that no matter what we talked about to her or even just Dad, it would suddenly be broadcast among the Scott clan or her own family, her daughters and siblings, with whom we had occasional contact. Eventually we learned only to share things with Dad and Rhonda if we didn't mind it getting out. But with Rhonda involved with Street Witches, let's just say the warning signs read "complicated."

"I bet Rhonda will have more to lose than you if she tells Dad. That's why they moved out of California anyway, so they wouldn't have to deal with us as much."

"You're probably right," Amber said, but she didn't look convinced. She then turned to Sister Lena and filled her in on our stepmother's visit.

"You know, if you'd like," the head witch offered, "the Street Witches can keep your stepmother busy while she's here. We have so many events, lectures, and activities, I bet we could fill her schedule so tight you'd hardly have to see her."

"See, Amber? No sweat," I said. "I bet after the first day she'll be dying to stay at the hotel so she doesn't have to put up with our chaos. And you know the pack and I would be happy to provide a little chaos for you. You need any landscaping done? Or you could finally enlarge your walk-in closet and that would make the guest room a catchall for all your clothes in the meantime. I bet Darcy would give you a discount; she still works at California Closets."

"I have been wanting more shoe space," she said wistfully.

"See, now there you go," I said, but I thought, *between witches, werewolves and wardrobe, I think we've got you covered.*

"So, the familiar communication spell..." Sister Lena said.

"And, once Amber does it, will I have my head to myself again?"

Sister Lena looked at me with a sad face and said, "No, sorry, ducks. I'm afraid you're stuck with him." She shrugged. "It's a dog thing."

*Hey! How did she know?* I thought, but I kept my mouth shut. Just another bullet point to add to "Ashlee's list of things she should probably learn about."

Amber pulled Lena aside as I got down to cleaning up after the witches. They were soon trickling out the door to wherever the night was calling them.

I heard the name Jeanetta Macdonald mentioned and pricked up my ears, sliding into a position I could see them. Sister Lena was speaking. "You know, we have sister witches who work in the prison system and it's their job to keep the paranormals under control. We don't talk about it much; it's like the underside of witchcraft, having to deal with those who abuse their powers. But we suppress their magic with various means, often by drugs that are administered to them in their food."

Funny, seemed to be a lot of that administering of potions going around. No wonder witches gained a reputation as poisoners. In fact, in that oft-quoted Bible verse, "Thou shalt not suffer a witch to live," the original Hebrew implied this was aimed at women who used herbs for ill: in other words, poisoners or purveyors of fell potions. Look at the witches in Sleeping Beauty or Snow White or a dozen other tales. What did they use? Poison and drugs. I didn't think these Street Witches were doing themselves any favors by imitating these methods.

On the other hand, I guess they do what they feel they gotta do.

Amber said, "Elle says that Jeanetta's still locked up tight, but I keep seeing her in my dreams, and today there were times during the ritual when I looked up and I could swear I saw her mocking face staring back at me. I'm worried, Lena."

Lena patted my sister's hand. "When I get home, I'll do a scrying spell and let you know what I find out. If Jeanetta's up to mischief, I'll know about it soon enough."

My twin hugged Lena and said her goodbyes.

"You never told me you were still getting visions of Jeanetta," I said after the door had shut.

"I didn't want you to worry."

"Well, I'm worried now," I said, and then sighed. "Just keep me in the loop, okay?"

"When I know, you'll know."

We both laughed.

That night, Amber did the spell. And you know me, little miss eavesdrop, I just had to listen in.

*Standard white poodle*
*You appear to be*
*Familiar spirit*
*Come to me*
*Siegfried. Daemon*
*Whatever you may be*
*Let your thoughts make sense to me*

It was surprisingly simple, Amber told me afterwards; again, no Grammy awards. As she already was psychic, she just had to open up her receptors to a different plane. So she wove a spell into a talisman and hung it on Ziggy's collar.

This meant if she wanted silence she could turn it off, like the twin bond. I couldn't help but wonder how Ziggy would do with it, two-way only when Amber wanted it. I mean, what type of a relationship is that when one party can just shut you out without any warning? But that's a witch and her familiar I guess. The witch is in charge, supposedly. And that was me and my sister too, sometimes, a constant dance of control and surrender. And we never knew which one of us was leading.

## 7

"So, what do you know about this Blood Moon Fever?" I asked Con Shelby over the phone the next day. It seemed safer that way, and hopefully wouldn't provoke my allergies.

"What do the pack elders say?"

"They don't seem worried about it at all. Says it's all superstition. But it sounds to me like a recipe for disaster if there's even a bit of truth to it."

"If it makes you feel any better I can make sure that no harm comes to you all. We can ask the witches for a spell, and I was already planning on calling in Adam and his team for security that night. We can have them loaded with tranq darts in case you all go, as you say, 'bat-shit crazy.'"

I could feel the air quotes over the phone. Sixth sense, women's intuition, or maybe I could just hear them.

"I give you my solemn oath and vow that I will do my utmost as your liege lord to keep you safe." Shelby oozed that magical charm and I sneezed. Sheesh. He must be strong if he could affect me like that over the phone. Better bookmark a conversation with a witch, I thought as I hung up on his assurances.

I saw my sister the next day as she headed out the door to take JR to swim practice.

"Oh, I heard from Sister Lena," she said as she gathered up her things from the vestibule.

"And…"

"And she said it's likely that Jeanetta's been trying to do spells from prison. She's been in and out of the infirmary with unexplained cuts and bruises and her normal handlers think that maybe some of the medications she's being given for pain are nullifying the effects of the drug suppressors. They say she's going in and out of trances, almost like a coma."

"That sounds ominous."

"Well, whatever it is, they say they're working on it."

"Good." One less thing out of my control to worry about, I thought and went to bone up on my homework.

The Delegation of Alphas showed up the following week. Two weeks until MoonFall. Why the hell were they going to be here for that long? Sigh. They did bring their own bitches, for which I was extremely thankful, plus an entourage of helpers, mostly omegas to do the scutwork.

I didn't need the unnecessary attention, but hell, they tried to give it to me anyway. *Lookie, a lupine!* Gag.

Con was hosting us all the first night at his home and it caught me off guard to be in the presence of so many alpha females. Honestly, it reminded me of high school. Mean girls.

"So, that's the little bitch who has Sierra's nips all in a twist," one among a chorus of voices sounded behind me, and afterward each new player cast her own judgment as I walked past them into the room. I tried to ignore them, but that only lasted for so long.

I wondered if all females had a similar scent, because below the lotions, creams and colognes there was a wild familiarity that had me on edge. The women were clustered around the sofas and decked out in everything from slacks to full-on evening attire, each with an attendant hovering like a medieval handmaiden.

I saw Dex Watley flirting with a couple of the attendants, making them laugh as was his wont, until their mistresses snarled at them.

At least I didn't feel out of place in the little black number I'd chosen, more like Holly Golightly in a den of cougars. I was one of the youngest females in attendance, except for a shy child who perched on the end of the far sofa in khaki cutoffs and a nondescript matching top, looking at me from under her dirty dishwater bangs with a hint of green eyes.

The men all loitered on the dais where the chapel altar had once stood and surveyed the landscape of a map that appeared to outline the Knightsbridge Canyon territory. They had manservants too. It was feeling quite crowded in here.

I slipped up beside Jackson and he took my hand and kissed me on the cheek. Will wasn't invited to this shindig, as he hadn't passed his rites of manly werehood or something. Though he wasn't happy about it, he tried to be graceful as I left him alone in my pool house with the remote this evening. I was actually relieved; I could see him starting something that would finish him, with all these much-more-experienced and dangerous wolves around.

Shelby raised his glass and clinked it with one of the many rings he wore, attracting everyone's attention. "Ladies and gentlemen, and I use those terms loosely, welcome to Knightsbridge Canyon, home of the new western addition. Tonight, we shall be formally recognizing the induction of a new pack of lycanthropes – and lupine, of course. Though I know you aren't all one hundred percent behind this experiment, we are honored that you came to visit our own little slice of California paradise. So, eat, drink, and be merry, for tomorrow we howl."

A few amused looks proceeded from the men, and titters from the women. I could tell some of the lycanthropes believed they were humoring Shelby in his role, as if he were a mere figurehead. Like powerful barons dealing with a weak king, they thought to further diminish his influence by showing barely concealed disrespect.

I wondered how that was going to play out.

When Shelby had finished with a few more blathering words, the women surrounded me like a gaggle of geese and I wondered what the next initiation rite would be. Did these people ever get tired of dominance games and just relax and let people be who they were?

"Don't take this wrong, but you smell amazing." A woman in a catsuit introduced herself as Danika Farkas, head bitch of the Yukon Territories.

"Why don't you ask her if you can taste her as well?" another said, holding out her hand to me. "Faolan Hemming. Grand Canyon Basin." I shook it firmly, wondering if she expected me to kiss her ring.

"Look honey," said an older, leather-skinned specimen from the Catalina Mountains above Tucson, hands on hips. "Don't let these bitches get to you. One of the good things about being an alpha female is there isn't anyone except your alpha male who can match you. And since we've already heard about how you put Sierra in her place, we just wanted to see for ourselves what the fuss is about."

So my reputation had preceded me. Great. I tried to be assertive without being aggressive, funny without being flippant, staring frankly around at the lot of them. "I'm no better than any of you, and no worse. With Sierra…well, I think I just wanted it more. That and she couldn't get over herself. I don't have that problem. That answer your question?" Wow, was I ever spinning it, downplaying my weaknesses and projecting strength – but that was how it was done.

My words seemed to satisfy them, for most of them lost interest soon enough. Showing no buttons to push was one of the basic solutions to potential bullies. Too strong a response and they win, because they got to you. Too weak a response and they win too, and they'll never let you alone. That left killing them or calmly facing them down.

I hoped I'd just done the latter.

The small talk dwindled as waiters and waitresses composed of Shelby's intimates made rounds with drinks and tapas plates filled with steak tartare, barely seared and seasoned miniature pork shanks, and for those who could stomach the stuff, various liver and organ meat *pâtés*. They tended to be too salty for my taste.

After declining several offers, I turned to find the girl – correction, the youngest alpha, probably still a teenager of nineteen-ish, invading my personal space with a sniff. "So, you're a lupine. You don't smell any different."

I stared down at the girl and flared my nostrils in return. I knew way more about her from one snootfull than I ever would have by interrogating her. Number one, she was quite pretty under that tangle of hair, and a virgin if I were to place a bet. She carried a plain, childlike beauty that threatened to blossom into strength and character if given a chance…assuming she survived. And although she had alpha written all over her, she was also beaten down and smelled familiar to me, but I couldn't quite place her. My wolf did, though and flashed me a picture of a silver-blond muzzle.

I suppressed a growl. Sierra. Wonder what this girl had to do with her? Was she friend or foe? Anyway, besides rabbit-trailing for a moment, I figured the girl's attempt at small talk was a rhetorical question and let her fumble her way forward. Hey, there was enough jockeying for position already among the doggie dignitary delegation. I didn't need to add to it by playing their game.

*Spit it out girl*, I thought, and then growled at her.

She got her courage underneath her and extended her hand. "I'm Colby. Colby Rio."

*She doesn't look like cheese,* I couldn't help but think. "Aren't you a little bit young for this crowd, Colby Rio? You appear to be what, eighteen and a couple MoonFalls?"

"Why? How old are you?"

Ah, the refreshing directness of the younger generation. I gave her my typical twenty-something answer, and then directed her back to the fact that she hadn't answered my question. Before she could, however, the hackles on the pelt of my wolf began to rise and I turned to find Sierra Layton framed in the doorway.

Sierra was my most recent nemesis. Okay, not really, but she was originally slated to be the female alpha of the Knightsbridge Canyon pack, until little ol' me got in the way and messed with the program. Sierra had tried to sabotage my standing until I sent her packing. I thought I was done with the bitch. Guess the universe had other ideas. The wolf inside me began to pace.

*Ashlee, what's wrong?* My sister's voice pierced my head and I opened up the bond to give her a visual. *I'm on my way.*

"Excuse me," I said to Colby as adrenaline shot through me. Jackson and I moved as one to brace Shelby in the kitchen, while Sully headed to the door to greet his daughter and hopefully remove her from my sight. This is one of those moments I wished that I was a witch, so I could zap her somewhere the sun don't shine.

"What is she doing here?" I practically shouted at the vampire as his thralls made themselves invisible out the back door.

Jackson put a hand on my arm. Touch has always seemed to calm me – as long as it's from a friend. Of course that little piece of enlightenment took a back seat to the fight-or-flight reaction I was trying to suppress. I felt like the Incredible Hulk as my shoulders started rising up to my ears.

"What happened to the banishment?" Jackson asked.

Shelby shrugged and shot his cuffs, picking a piece of imaginary lint from one. "It comes as a surprise to me as well. I just found out myself from Antonio Pallermo. Sierra challenged the Rio's bitch for territory and won. Killed her, in fact, which is a bit much, hmm? As she's now female alpha of Coeur d'Alene, she's a dignitary. That means she has diplomatic immunity. I can't change that."

"You know, you're a snake don't you?" I said. "You could have warned us right away. Sent us a text…something."

"And spoil the entertainment? Besides, this isn't my problem unless you make it so. If you want to be an alpha, grow up and be one. It's not all about being the strongest. Sometimes it's about being the bigger person." He smiled, showing his fangs. "Or faking it."

*Touché*, I thought. I had a feeling I was going to try to kill this vampire someday, but not today. I shook my head and left Jackson to fight it out with Con. I just wasn't up to the confrontation. It's not in my nature to run from a battle, but somehow he always made me feel like I was back in school with the teachers wagging their fingers at me.

*We wrestle not with flesh and blood*, the catechism came to me, only the guy who wrote that didn't know that there were worse things in flesh and blood than he imagined. No, nothing trumps the darkness that dwelt in the human heart. Trap it in a supernatural body and it became much more terrifying.

No, not talking about Con.

Me.

I was a dangerous bitch, and Sierra made me want to give the rage its freedom, but I tried to be at least half a grownup here. If I couldn't be calm in her presence, then I just wouldn't be anywhere near her. I slammed out the kitchen door and into the alcove with bay seats and windows where we'd left our purses. The wait staff scattered back inside to do their jobs.

Colby caught up with me. "I'm sorry about Sierra. She's always doing things like that. Anything to get your goat and make you feel inferior. Anyway, she's why I'm here." Colby pointed back through the doorway in Sierra's direction, and her finger exuded animosity.

I knew the feeling.

I couldn't help myself. I joined Colby at the doorjamb and together we peeked out from the dimness to watch the scene. Sullivan must have given his child a dressing-down, as I caught the tail end of his admonishment for Sierra to inhabit her new position like he'd taught her, with grace and nobility.

Sierra squared her shoulders and regally swept into the room with her eyes raised, her coat of animal furs, utterly improbable in this weather, barely clearing the door's frame. A much older man also dripping in furs followed her. At least he wasn't over-accessorized. Sierra was adorned with diamonds.

"That's my new stepmother," Colby said, eyes glazed.

"I'm so sorry," I said. I held my hand to my chest and commenced impromptu meditative breathing. The tension went up in the main room as the rest of the wolves caught a whiff of me. I tried to bite back my homicidal tendencies and lower the psychological pressure.

"Me too," Colby said. "She's beyond a bitch. And that's my dad. I would call him a coldhearted bastard, but he's the only blood kin I've got left. Del Monte Rio, head of the Coeur d'Alene pack."

"Why in God's name did your father marry Sierra?" I spoke through gritted teeth that I was trying not to grind. *I'm handling this surprisingly well*, I lied to myself. As long as she stayed on that side of the room, I'd keep my distance as well. Although, my wolf gave me an internal visual of vultures circling carrion.

"Sierra challenged and killed my last stepmom, who wasn't a lot better, to tell you the truth. After my real mom was killed, every subsequent alpha female became Mrs. Del Monte Rio. Dad's a traditionalist. That's how it was done in the old days; you know, when nobody lived together without getting married. So that's how it's done now. The gospel according to Del Monte."

"Sounds like he's selling canned vegetables."

"You have no idea how much he hates jokes like that."

"And now you're stuck with her," I said. Yup, that's me. Cut to the chase and pull no punches.

A pained expression crossed Colby's face, but she shrugged and said, "Par for the course."

"How many stepmothers have you had?" I asked.

"Sierra's like, my fifth. Or is it fourth?" She counted on her fingers. "No, five."

"Why, so many?"

"You know, for a female alpha you don't know much about our ways, do you?"

I kept my tone even, nonreactive. She was only a kid, after all. "I didn't grow up with pack. I'm not even a lycanthrope; haven't you heard? I'm the ultimate black sheep, if wolves were sheep. Everybody wants me, everybody hates me, guess I'll go eat worms."

Colby turned her hooded eyes to mine. "I think we're both weirdos."

I hugged her then, feeling very big-sisterly. "Cool. We'll be weirdos together."

The girl sniffed. "Are those cloves I smell in your purse?"

I gripped the clutch in mock concern and said with a grin, "Maybe…"

"Please, please, please, let's go have a smoke. It's getting too stuffy in here and I am *so* not ready to face the step-monster."

"Me neither," I said, but she knew what I meant.

We beat a quick retreat out a side door and stood in the chapel garden that connected to the small cemetery and soon were sucking on glowing smoke-sticks in the dusk of evening.

Colby said, "You should know that to most were-wolves, Knightsbridge is a joke. A gay male alpha, I mean. C'mon. This is bucking tradition in a huge way, far worse than with mundane society. And from what I gather, since you're probably the only female lupine alpha in existence,

I bet they've been keeping you in the dark about pretty much everything."

I'd surmised as much, but with my socially liberal leanings and the outdated ways of pack tradition, I'd figured the less I knew the better, and didn't ask. Out of sight, or smell, and out of mind. Where the hell was my journalistic edge? Oh right, it had been bought off by massage therapists and exfoliating scrubs. I tried to stay away from subjects such as politics and religion in my regular life, but I guess lycanthrope history was something I ought to bone up on. I took a long drag of the clove. "Go on."

"You know, most alphas win the right to dominate in battle, usually to submission but sometimes to death. The younger generation isn't as bloodthirsty as the old, but unless the previous alpha is willing to leave or take a subservient role, death is usually the best answer – especially if the wolf is old."

"Sounds rough."

"Times were tougher back then, Dad says. They used to burn us out with torches and pitchforks. Sometimes we'd have to kill them, whole villages even. Nowadays, people either think we're cool and we incorporate them, or they don't want to believe their own eyes anyway. That's what the fangs are for. Keep the sheep loyal or scrub their memories."

She said it like it was nothing, but it made me profoundly uncomfortable. Good thing weres were mostly immune to vampire mind magic.

"It's pretty great what you're doing here. I sure hope it works out," she went on, taking a deep drag.

I wondered for a moment what she thought the great part was, but I didn't ask. If knowledge was power, I just realized, I must be an idiot savant.

"That doesn't explain why you're here," I steered her back to the subject at hand. Guess I wasn't the only bitch who went spoor-sniffing.

"Well, though I'm old enough to breed, Dad's never let any of the pack get near me during MoonFall, or frankly at any other time of the day or night. I've had bodyguards since I was twelve years old. We're Catholic, so Dad's kept me locked up tighter than the Vatican. You may not be able to see it, but I have an invisible chastity belt that makes the President's Secret Service look like rent-a-cops. He tried to send me to an Inuit community of lycanthrope females, but that only made me bi-curious and when he got wind of that, I was on a flight back to Idaho. Now he's decided to send me here."

"Here? You're not just visiting?"

"If I were being nice I'd say I think he knows deep down that pretty soon I won't be his little girl anymore. If I wanted to be fair, I'd say he's getting old and tired of watching me like a hawk and he's letting me go. If I wanted to be mean, though, I'd say Sierra's got him bewitched and he's throwing me out so he can use up the last bit of juice in him screwing his trophy wife. Who knows? I might get a half-sibling or two out of the deal, though I hate to think how they'll turn out with Sierra as a mother."

"Well, the silver lining is, you'll have a lot more freedom here. But you won't be the alpha." I narrowed my eyes at her. "Unless that's your goal?"

"If I ever want to be an alpha, I promise I'll find somewhere else to challenge," she replied, holding up a forefending hand. "I don't want to be the one that killed the magic lupine, after all."

"Oh, that's all that's holding you back?"

Colby hugged me again. "No, Ashlee. I'll never kill you. I like you."

"Good to hear." I hugged her back, and it felt good. I wish I'd had a little sister.

A man's voice sounded behind me and we both started, dropping our cigarettes to the ground and grinding them out with our heels as we saw who it was.

"Del Monte Rio." The man extended his hand.

"Daddy," Colby said and gave him a quick but strained hug.

His nostrils flared at the lingering smoke, but he refrained from voicing the judgment I saw there.

"I may not agree with my daughter's choices," – he put emphasis on the word "choices" like there was some extra meaning there, maybe about her sexuality – "but that doesn't mean I love her any less. At least with Jackson, I know she'll be taken care of if she finds herself in a womanly way."

Colby sighed. "Daddy, why can't you just say 'pregnant'? You're too old-fashioned. Maybe Sierra can drag you into the twenty-first century."

Pregnant? With Jackson? As in, wolf pups? So Colby was Jackson's wolf answer to my relationship with Will, and damned if I wasn't unnerved at the thought. Though why should I be? It made perfect sense.

Yeah, sure.

Rio's broad shoulders lifted as he took a deep breath preparatory to raising his voice, I could tell, and my brain began jumping through hoops and my heart started racing. It was entirely too much like what my own father had done during my childhood, when getting ready to deliver a stern lecture backed up by an application of the belt.

I could feel the onslaught of an anxiety attack and was afraid that when my head finally wrapped around the information I'd just received, I wasn't going to be suitable company for anyone, let alone a pack of doggie dignitaries. "If you'll excuse me," I said, "I need to get some air." Since we were already outside that seemed redundant, but I had to place some distance between myself and this new information. I threaded my way through the cemetery just as Amber pulled up at the curb.

"Get in," she said as she reached across and opened the passenger door for me. I dove in, buckled up and Amber raced away. We could see Jackson, Sully and the rest of the Knightsbridge Canyon pack piling out of the rectory as if to come after me. When they saw I was with Amber, they stopped. Well, that was a bit weird. Showed how much they thought of me, as a piece of chattel rather than a free person.

"Breathe. Ashlee. Breathe," Amber said and shoved a covered plastic bottle at me. "Drink this."

It was the tea of tranquility. My eyes teared up and I choked out an ironic gasp of disbelief. I downed the tea as

Amber blasted Goddess worship music at me. Ziggy stuck his head between the seats and pushed it into my lap. Seriously, if I didn't laugh, I'd cry and I was so not going to let this whole thing get the best of me. And I have to tell you, there are some really good praise choruses to the Divine Feminine out there. But you might have to join Spotify to find them. Although I think Amber has Sirius XM. Or maybe just casual XM.

Anyway, we drove up the Canyon and when I'd calmed down enough, Amber began to talk. "Will wanted to come but Siegfried wouldn't let him."

I looked a question at her.

"Yes, we're talking now."

*I have an enchanted collar,* the familiar thought at me, thought at us both.

"So, what's going on?"

"Don't you know already?" I petted Ziggy's head.

"I know Sierra's back in town and I got that you can't do anything but ride it out till she's gone. But something hit you especially hard just as I arrived. Something about your wolf and the puppies. I told you, you need to reconsider this."

"I'm not reconsidering having the puppies," I muttered. "I'm just reconsidering the father."

"You and Will having problems?"

You know how sometimes if you talk long enough you stumble upon your own answers. Well, that wasn't this time. If I was going to be honest with myself – and the only person I'm starting to believe you owe full honesty to is yourself – the truth was, though I chose

Will, my wolf wanted Jackson. And the wolf was me, wasn't it? Freaky Friday!

"Sounds like you have another decision to make."

"Another?" I wasn't sure what my twin was referring to.

"You said you were going to hold off on the puppies. This just gives you more reason to. I mean, what do you know about what you're getting yourself into? Trying to fulfill some goofy prophecy about uniting the supernatural kingdoms."

"What? I'm not trying to – where the hell did you get that from?" I demanded as she pulled up to the trailhead to Lover's Leap.

"I sent you my research."

"I haven't had a chance to get to it yet!"

"I swear Ashlee, if you would just take that analytical eye and journalistic integrity you use when writing your articles and apply them to your own life, you would be *so* much farther ahead of the game than you are now."

"Yes, well, we wouldn't want to mess up that dark mirror you've got hidden in your pool house." I know, it was a poor metaphor, but I wasn't thinking straight.

Amber sighed. "I packed you a bag of clothes." She motioned toward the back seat. "GPS, bottled water, raw hamburger. I figured you'd want a run the way you were feeling when I caught your distress call."

"I didn't call...never mind," I said and exited the car. I opened the back door and Ziggy hopped out with my gym bag in his mouth.

*No, you're not coming,* I thought at him.

"Siegfried will wait for you and guard your clothing. Just make sure you clip the GPS receiver to your collar."

"I *have* done this before, you know," I told her through the open window.

She smiled. "Shake it off, Ashlee," she said. *Or run it off. Whatever.* She blasted Taylor Swift out the window as she left Ziggy and me in the dust.

I looked at the dog-daemon. "Bet you never thought you'd be twin-sitting."

Thankfully, and wisely, he kept his reply to himself as we headed up the canyon.

## 8

I learned this from Jackson later:

After I'd left, small talk had ensued until the twelve-course meal in tapas had the rest of the delegation reclining or sitting on the scattered chaise lounges, leather La-Z-Boys and love seats. Someone mentioned the Blood Moon fever, about which a semi-heated debate ended with a consensus. A few of the young alphas disagreed, but the majority of elder voices held sway. Everyone would have to refrain from mating.

Sister Lena had petitioned the delegation with the proposal that her people cast a spell to keep the Blood Moon fever from doing harm to any sentient being in Knightsbridge and, though many thought that the witches' fears were unfounded, it seemed like it couldn't hurt.

Shelby topped the day off by driving the entire delegation out, in limousines of course, to a ranch he owned on the eastern ridge of Mount Rettig in order to provide livestock in a confined area. The weres all stripped naked under the moon, turned, and feasted to their wolfish hearts' content. Can't have the locals opening hunting season because we were poaching their livestock, after all.

I had to give him kudos; hey, it was a good decision. Maybe Peg was a good influence on Shelby, teaching the Con-man how to be more human.

Naw, he was still a snake. I'm sure it was purely self-serving.

"Hey, Ziggy?" I consciously spoke directly to the familiar instead of the poodle for the first time in a week.

*Yes, milady,* he responded, trotting up to me and attempting to gnaw on my fingers. Guess he was feeling pretty lonely since I'd been ignoring him, so it seemed he didn't care what I called him, as long as I called him. Ugh. Some dogs can be so needy. Hmm. Irony?

"Ew, gross. Knock it off," I told him. He sat on his haunches, cocked his head to the right and stared at me. "You know, you're not helping your case, looking all cute in that doggy way. Not if you want to be taken seriously as a familiar instead of a dog."

*Just keeping in practice.*

"So, I was thinking about how Amber can't see our mom and I can, and I was wondering if there was a spell that would allow her to see and hear her like I can." I wanted to do something nice for Amber since she'd come through for me the other night.

Ziggy thought for a minute.

*We could do a spell to let her see and hear ghosts, but it's not that particular and I don't know if she wants to become a ghost whisperer. Besides, it wouldn't last. Psychics deal more with time, cause and effect, potentiality and that rot. It would probably open her up to all sorts of influences.*

"Yeah, she'd love that. NOT. Anything else you can think of?"

*She could do a ride-along spell.*

"That sounds interesting. What's that?"

*It's a spell that allows a witch to share the consciousness of another being. She'd be like an observer sitting on your shoulder, only in the back of your head. Of course, during which time she'd be seeing what you see and hearing what you hear.*

"That sounds perfect. As long as it's temporary." The thought of Amber forever in my head even more than she already was…yikes.

*It has some side effects. A few drawbacks, depending on your perspective.*

"Such as?"

*Such as, anything you think, she has access to, and vice versa. You won't be able to block each other for the duration.*

"Well, she always said she wished she knew what it was like to be me."

*You must know, there is risk involved.*

"What kind of risk?"

*Well, for the time she's in your head, her body will be comatose. As long as you get her back into her own body within a specified amount of time, it will be just like she went into a deep coma, and then woke up. But, you might want to have an IV on hand in case something goes wrong. If her spirit doesn't get back, she'll need life support.*

We told Amber about our idea and she seemed skeptical, but curious. Granted, it was a little scary to think about putting my twin sister into a coma, but it was only temporary, right? Ziggy assured her that it was a spell most witches got around to eventually, wanting to know what it's like to do a ride-along with their familiar, for example.

Elle was adamantly against it, and tensions ran high in the Gordon-Scott household until I suggested that Amber call another gathering of the Street Witches to the house and they could mentor her on the process.

Ziggy was a bit miffed that his mentorship wasn't enough, but Elle was a hard sell on anything that put Amber in danger, to which I threw in my final card and promised that Will's sister Samantha would be on hand as backup medical treatment.

Besides, this would just be a trial run, riding along with Ziggy, a friendly being. Not that Amber and I wouldn't be friendly, but, well, you never know how ugly it could get with two of us in there, right?

All bases covered.

They do say the road to hell is paved with good intentions. But I'll get to that.

We sent JR to his dad's and gathered the usual suspects, plus a few extras.

There was Sister Lena, Sister Nayala, Sister Bertrille and an Abbess Layolin to call the corners and sweep the space clean from negative energy. There was Ziggy and Spanky and me, of course. Ghost Mom, who was beaming with excitement.

Will's sister, Samantha, who I'm only just lately finding out is much more informed than we ever would have guessed, had oxygen, shock paddles, and an IV drip on hand, while Elle sat stoically on the edge of the bed, holding my sister's hand as she reclined among the pillows like Cleopatra.

Surprisingly enough, we were all crammed into the master bedroom, a sacred space that even JR and I couldn't enter without explicit permission. No wonder both my twin and her wife appeared vulnerable. This was a huge concession on my sister's part and I marveled at the changes she was making to even explore a new aspect of her neo-witchy self.

The witches called the directions and invoked the Goddess to midwife their "sister" into the heart of the familiar, which was funny, because as I understood it, the ride-along spell was a brain thing. Ziggy used the analogy of the conscious observer, an almost pure non-judgmental consciousness that one could inhabit in the practice of mindfulness. Only this conscious observer was more like the peanut gallery.

Anyway, I was glad I wasn't in for the trial run, So, I could spectate and take notes. I wanted to record it on my cell phone, but Amber nixed that one.

"Knowing you, the damn thing would end up somewhere on YouTube." To which I vehemently replied that I might think about it but I'd like to think that my good sense would get the better of me. Regardless, as it stood I was stuck with my favorite gel ink pen and composition notebook. I'm good at taking notes. Making sense of them on the other end, now that's a whole 'nother story.

*Siegfried, come*, my sister thought at the dog, and he gracefully leaped up to lie down next to my sister on the ridiculously huge California King. She placed her hand on his head and turned to the witches. "I'm ready."

Sam pricked Amber's finger with a lancet and pressed the blood spot just above Ziggy eyes, halfway between his ears, the drying rust color like a blemish on the dog's lambswool coat.

"Good thing we only have to do that once," Amber said, sucking on her finger. Sometimes she was such a wimp. Then she began to sing the chant she'd been taught.

I felt a chill run down my spine and a lump rise in my throat at the intimacy of the moment. Except for the sound of Ziggy dog-crooning next to her, the house was eerily silent.

*Bring my consciousness to bear*
*Upon my chosen familiar*
*Canine thoughts and canine sight*
*Be my refuge for a night*

She sang it like a round, or a chant, evoking a resonance of our childhood growing up with a mother who bought us DVDs of Mister Rogers' Neighborhood and Romper Room and Captain Kangaroo, all the old stuff from her own time as a little girl. In fact, I think the tune she was using was similar to the one about the magic mirror.

I must have dozed off, because, *Mom*, was the next thing I remember hearing and my eyelids shot open and Ziggy was off the bed and prancing around with our ghostly mother. He'd tackled her to the floor and she took on a solidity I'd never seen as she sank to lotus position and took Ziggy and my sister's consciousness into her arms.

Elle gasped and I realized that Ghost Mom was no longer invisible to everyone else. My sister crooned with Ziggy's mouth and Annabelle Scott spoke sweet nothings into the familiar's ear.

"Why don't we leave the girls to their reunion," Nurse Sam said and ushered the rest of us out of the room, but I wasn't too upset, werewolf hearing and all. Besides, with Amber's body in a coma it seemed that the twin bond was wide open and I could see through Ziggy's eyes myself. I had to lie down against the nausea I felt at the superimposition, so I retired to the floor of the guest bedroom and turned all the lights out.

My mother's frame wavered before me on the cinema in my mind and she rose, Ziggy-Amber attached to her hip, and approached Elle who still sat on the edge of the bed. "Elle Gordon. I am so desperately pleased to finally meet you," Annabelle said and held out her hand.

Elle looked at it and then extended her left hand toward my Mother's right. Annabelle caught it and brought it to her lips and I shivered as the scent of Jean Nate wrapped around us. Ghost Mom was bringing them all together.

"If you'll pardon me, Mrs. Scott," Elle said, "but how can you be here?"

"I only get a few dispensations in my role as guardian of lost souls, but I wanted to meet the woman who made my daughter happy."

"You know, I think your daughter would appreciate this moment more if she weren't stuck in a dog's body."

*I keep telling them I'm not a dog.*

I laughed at the absurdity of it all.

Ghost Mom said, "You're absolutely right." And the next thing I knew, Amber was popped back into her own body, the twin bond was shut down, and I got my equilibrium back.

*Ghost Mom has powers*, I thought, but I felt a bit hurt until Ziggy relayed that my mother only had a limited time to take advantage of the energies of a full manifestation. Besides, she wasn't going anywhere.

I decided to leave them alone and go for a run up the canyon. I reminded myself of one of the things that all the twin books I've read said was important: parents needed to establish individual relationships with each of the twins. I've had Ghost Mom for years. Amber, on the other hand, was making up for lost time. I could be the grownup here and let them have each other all to themselves for a while.

At dawn the next morning, I found Amber sitting out on the back porch with her coffee. She looked like she'd been up all night, but she was radiant.

"So, how was it?" I asked.

"I've always envied you, you know. You seemed to get most of her attention."

"Yes, but you were Daddy's little girl."

"The price of that was too high," she said, referring to Dad's long, painful and not-really-over period of adjustment when she finally came out of the closet. Amber always told me, "You know, I never really felt like a lesbian. I just fell in love with a woman."

"And now?" I asked.

"I still envy you. Not quite as much."

We both chuckled.

"So, tell me. What did she say?"

Amber looked at me and said, "That's for me to know, and you to never, *ever* find out."

"Hey, no fair!"

"We're not kids anymore, Ashlee. We don't have to share everything."

And though I knew she was right, it felt like something inside of me died a little.

If this is what growing up feels like, I don't wanna.


"What died in here?" I voiced to nobody as I opened up the shed in which Elle kept her toys and the smell of rotting meat wafted out. I'd gone to get a couple of seahorses, er, sawhorses, so I could do some silk painting

"Don't let the flies in!" My sister called out the window and reinforced her words over the twin bond we shared.

*That's the titan arum, the corpse flower, and it's for the spell we're doing to protect you all over the Blood Moon.*

I closed and locked the shed, but not before a waiting swarm of big ugly black insects made it into the aluminum building. *Hope that's not going to cause a huge problem,* I thought. I'd decided I needed to save a little face with the delegation and give them all hand-made silk scarves that I dyed and set myself. Well, all the females at least. I could do four at a time, which means I could have them done in two days. Dying silk is a messy business, but besides my writing it was the one thing I could always rely on. In silk painting, even my mistakes came out beautiful.

Will had cobbled together an old water heater down in the basement and I could steam-set the silks after they were dry and wrapped in newsprint.

I wonder if I should think about dyeing more, as a moneymaking cottage industry? Get it, cottage? Never mind. I set up in an undeveloped flat of land between the shed and a copse of trees that bordered the back of the property and began the arduous process of using push pins to stretch the silk over the bars.

Soon I was laying down my patterns with a blue fabric pen that would wash out later. So, I was up to the elbows of my smock in multicolored spillage when Colby showed up in the backyard. I only got the heads-up a moment before when Amber opened up the twin bond in my head and spat, *this isn't Grand Central station, Ashlee. You need to tell me when someone is coming over, or at least tell them to come in by the gate and not make me answer the door.*

*Hey, I didn't know myself!*

But she'd already shut the bond down.


"What's that godawful smell?" Colby asked as she passed by the shed.

"Corpse flower. Witchy stuff. Blood Moon Spell. That's all I know."

"Huh," she said and looked at the scarves that were drying in their stretcher bars against the back fence. "Those are cool. What are they?"

"Silk scarves for the delegates. The bitches, anyway."

"Cool! I want that one," she said and pointed to a teal number I was particularly fond of. On all of the scarves I'd used a gouda, which in this case is not a cheese, but a rubberized liquid that hardens into a flexible but impenetrable line to create a resist and stop the bleed. I never treated my silks beforehand, and in these I'd sketched paw print indentations over a multi-colored backdrop that evoked nature in rich fall and autumn colors.

"No worries. It's yours," I said, pleased at her enthusiasm. I didn't paint silk often, but scarves made the best presents at Christmas time.

"Awesome…anyway, I know it's not polite to show up unannounced, but after the other night and the fiasco that I caused –"

I interrupted, "You didn't cause a fiasco. You just gave me more information than I was willing to handle at the time."

"That's me, Queen of TMI."

I laughed. "That's what Amber used to say about me."

"So, you're okay?" Her eyes pled her case.

I sighed.

"You're okay with Jackson and me?" Colby pressed.

"The wolf in my head may want Jackson," I confessed, "but the heart of the human knows Will is the only alpha male for me."

"But, I thought Will was a beta."

*Ah, the literal teenager, always trying to sharpshoot her elders.* "It's just a figure of speech."

"Can I ask you a personal question?"

"Depends on how personal."

"When did you first have sex?"

"As a wolf or as a human?"

"Both."

"Human? High School. Wolf? Never."

"OMG! You're a virgin too? Did they keep you locked up like me?"

I laughed at that. "Only one who locks me up is me."

"What does that mean?"

"Nothing." I said. This child did not need me to give her a lecture on consensuality and velvet handcuffs. Besides, chances are she'd already read Fifty Shades of Grey. "It means most of the time we're complicit in our confinement."

"I don't get it."

"Well, you're eighteen now, and you're here. You can disregard whatever restrictions your father put on you any time, right?"

"I guess. Daddy gave me the key to the chastity belt. I can take it off any time now."

"But will you?"

"I don't know. Maybe. Eventually."

I lifted my palm in a there-you-go gesture. "Like I said. You're complicit."

She thought about that for a while. I let her mull it over.

"So, Jackson said you have a cage in your basement and Dad and Sierra wanted to know if I could use it over MoonFall."

"He said that, eh?" I was hot after working all afternoon on the dyeing, so I splashed myself with the garden hose. I guess I wasn't thinking too much about teenagers and hormones, because Colby's eyes got wide as the water, well, let's say it highlighted my better assets. "Er, sorry."

"No worries," she squeaked out. "Sully also said it might be good to have the ulv on hand with me, just in case."

"Not ready to do the deed, yet, eh?" I asked, tactlessly.

"I'm just trying to get my bearings. Jackson thinks I should have sex as a human before I try it as a lycanthrope. Especially not over the Blood Moon."

"What? Gotta test drive the Honda before you go for the Lamborghini?"

"What's a Lamborghini?"

Can you say "sheltered"? I was seriously going to have to show this kid Fast and Furious. We could have a marathon and watch every single movie. How many were there, nineteen by now? "Never mind. So, what do you think?"

"I don't know. I used to think I wanted to get it over with. But now I'm thinking I should at least be in love with a guy before we knock boots."

"And when you say sex, you mean…" I hedged.

"Everything. Nothing."

"So you've never even…"

"Dad would never let me. Only thing he let me do was kiss and hold hands. He would have killed anyone he smelled had tried to go too far."

"But what about the Inuits?"

"Dad said what a girl does with another woman doesn't count."

"I think my sister would beg to differ on that one."

*Ashlee!* My sister's voice resounded in my head. *Don't you dare put words in my mouth!*

*Then you get out here and talk to this child!*

Silence. Opening up the twin bond between us had its pros and cons. I guess I glamorized the experience in hindsight, the feeling of connection and energy that flowed between us when the floodgates were wide open. But it often meant a lack of privacy and left me with a hollow feeling when she shut it down. Did that make me codependent?

"Anyway, Jackson said you'd be a good person to talk to about all of this stuff."

I rolled my eyes. "Remind me to thank him for that."

"I really like him," Colby said. "I mean, he's like twice my age, but Dad said except for his being gay, he's like the perfect alpha."

"I wouldn't go that far, but he is quite the gentleman." I surveyed my handiwork one last time, before I went to wash up. "Well, come on. I'll show you the layout."

We went into the pool house and down into the basement. I ditched my dirty clothes onto the washer and pulled a robe around myself, and then I showed her the cage with water dispenser and food bowls and the bedding, and the secret panel that opened up to the tunnel leading to the duck blind. "There are chains. But I don't leave them lying out."

"I've stayed in worse," she said.

"Where are you staying now anyway? I mean, if you're coming here to live."

"Oh, I'm over at the lodge on the lake, but they're talking about moving up to the ridge in the ranch house. I mean, Master Shelby hired a caretaker for the place, but Sully wants to bring some of his livestock and horses in from Montana. I love to ride."

"I'm surprised the horses let you ride them."

"They're special horses."

My brain took a leap of imagination and I watched a naked Jackson riding off into the sunset on horseback, but what I said was, "Boy, am I out of the loop." I determined to rectify that situation after the doggie delegation was gone.

We went back upstairs and I made some coffee. We sat down at my kitchenette table.

"It must be weird being the only one of your kind," Colby said.

"I'm not the only one of my kind. Otherwise no one would know anything about me." *I can't be,* I thought. A girl could die of terminal uniqueness.

"The only documented one, then. That we know of in modern times."

"Oh, I have documents now? I'd like to see those. Am I pure-bred?" I sighed and wondered if I were getting too comfortable. Letting others make a lot of decisions for me. I mean, I thought that I'd regained a modicum of control when Will took the bite and became a lycanthrope. But the pack itself still needed to reproduce in its own way. "So, how'd you get here?"

"Master Shelby has several cars, and I borrowed one with a driver. He'll come pick me up when I call or text him, although I think he's parked near the irrigation ditch down the street listening to an audiobook. He's kind of cute, for an intimate, and he says it's a great way to pass the time."

"What, being an intimate?"

"No, audiobooks. Duh."

Funny that sex-mad teens still missed the sex jokes. I guess I was too subtle.

I heard a knock at my door, and then my sister turned the knob and stuck her head in the crack. "Ashlee, why don't you and your guest come to the main house for dinner?" She suggested this in that tone where you knew it wasn't a suggestion.

"Sure," I said, glancing at Colby.

That seemed to be the signal for my sister to enter. "I'm Amber," she said and stuck out her hand. "Sorry I wasn't here to greet you earlier. My son John Robert was the one who met you at the door."

"Colby Rio." She clasped my sister's hand, looking back and forth from me to her as if to compare.

"I'm assuming chicken is okay."

"Uh, sure."

"As long as I don't have to chase it down," I said.

Amber shot me *the look*. "Colby, why don't you come with me while Ashlee showers and we can get to know each other? I'll introduce you to Spanky and Siegfried." *And for God's sake Ashlee, put on some clothes. I don't have your wolf's hearing and even I can hear Colby's heart palpitations. It's not fair to dangle red meat in front of a hungry wolf and then say no, so unless you want to go there, stop teasing the girl.*

*Hey, feel free to make her fantasies come true,* I shot back.

Amber made a strangled sound in her throat and led the child out the door.

I applied myself to the three S's – shower, shampoo, and shave the legs – and forced myself to dress like a grown-up.

Sigh. I'd rather be naked.

"You're going to live up on the hill with a couple of gay men and a pack of werewolves?" my sister exclaimed at Colby over dinner. "Absolutely not! You should stay with us."

I looked at my twin sister in shock. This was *so* not normal. I pinged on the twin bond to get her attention, which was something I was only lately learning to do. Though I sometimes resented his being in my head, Ziggy was proving to be quite the teacher in spite of his silly poodle ways.

Amber looked at me slyly but shook her head. Elle was even looking at her like she'd grown a second one. Obviously, she was up to something and I guess I'd just have to wait to find out.

I didn't have to wait long.

"Um. I'm flattered," Colby mumbled over the corn on the cob she was gnawing on. My sister put another napkin down next to her and she grabbed at it like a life preserver. "But, I'll have to ask my father and get permission from the pack."

"Why do you have to ask your father?" I said.

"Because I just do, all right? At least while he's still in town."

This girl really needed to grow a pair.

Ziggy stuck his nose in my crotch and I grabbed his muzzle underneath the table, which is what he wanted as he began licking the butter juice off my fingers.

*The child doesn't know it yet, but she just became interference for when your stepmother is here,* Ziggy commented.

Okay, maybe talking to my sister's familiar wasn't all bad. I looked at Amber with a new appreciation. "I still don't think he looks like a Siegfried," I said, dropping into my old habit of trying to have the last word.

She smirked at me. "Siegfried. Don't beg," she said, for Colby's benefit. "I'm sure they'll say its fine. We girls need to stick together. And we've got plenty of room.

Have you thought about a job? We could always use a live-in kid-sitter."

*You do know that Colby's a lycanthrope, right?* I thought at her.

She shrugged. *What's another werewolf in the family?*

*You were all twisted up about me living across the lawn from JR and now you want Colby to stay inside the house?*

*I just said that. I know you'd never hurt JR.*

I shook my head at Amber's contradictions. *You sure Elle is going to be on board with this?*

*She will be.*

I always assumed that a mature relationship would be manifest in compromise, but ever since I can remember it felt like my sister always got her way. Maybe they compromised in the bedroom, I thought, and then shut the twin bond down. My sister gave me a look that said *Seriously? You went there?*

Colby and I started clearing the table while Elle and Amber retired to their bedroom to "have a talk."

At dinner up at the ranch house on Friday night I presented the scarves, wrapped in foil gift boxes, to the ladies of the delegation. I even gave one to Sierra. It would have been déclassé to do otherwise.

She looked like she didn't know what to do with it, but followed suit as the rest of the women put the packages in their purses. I wasn't good at small talk, but the scarves gave me a chance to tell them a little bit about my hobby. They were gracious and my estimation of the doggie dignitaries rose, with the one obvious exception.

Most expressed regrets that Colby wouldn't be with them during MoonFall, but secretly all envied her the chance to pioneer a new kind of regime. They may have convinced themselves that they were satisfied with pack status quo, but everyone wanted something unique and, presumably, better, for their daughters and sons.

As the newest and lowest in established status, Sierra mostly stayed silent among these bitches. When she did try to speak, they verbally wolf-packed her until she bared her metaphorical throat and slunk away. Danika even pulled me aside and let me know that as far as they were concerned, I was the wounded party to Sierra's prior shenanigans.

My impression of these women went up a couple of notches and I found myself grateful and humbled by their perceptiveness. It was like we were the Astronaut Wives Club and I was Annie Glenn, the one with the invisible stutter.

Oh, well. If different meant special, I was riding the short bus and happy to do it.

The evening waned and we all looked toward the waxing moon, itching to shed our human skins and run free. The menfolk had left us to it and we took advantage of the night to shift and hunt rabbits that had been released before we'd gotten there.

"Hi," Amber said in my head, and I realized something was different.

"This ain't the twin bond."

"I did the ride-along spell, just for a little while."

"On me?"

"No, on myself, silly. You're just the target."

Exasperation. "That's what I meant. This is really rude, you know, jumping into my head without permission."

"You can always block me out."

"How?"

"I'm not sure."

I stuck my fingers in my ears. "Om mani padme hum…om mani padme hum…"

"It's not working."

"So you lied about me being able to block you?"

"No, that's just what Siegfried told me."

"Guess I'll have to get him to teach me how to do it." I sighed. "It's okay for now."

She gave me a running commentary on the experience of turning and being a wolf for the first time – for her – until she realized that we actually were going to kill and eat the bunnies. Then she blinked out with a final "Ew," and good riddance.

This made me think of a traumatic episode from when we were little, maybe three or four years old. Mornings we went to Happy Tyme Day Care and Preschool to give my mother a break from toting around four children – Amber, me, Adam and Whelan. They had gentle angora rabbits there, pets for the kids.

One morning we arrived to the horrific sight of rabbit parts and broken cages and bright red blood on earth tone fur. They said it was wild dogs, but now I wondered.

It didn't bother me as much as it had Amber. I was always the tomboy, she the girly-girl.

Afterward, we shifted back and used the rough open showers installed in the back of the barn. Lots of good naked woman flesh. Amber would be disappointed she'd cut out so quickly.

Colby looked like she'd seen it all before and she wasn't staring at me anymore. I guess it's true what they say, that a little bit of strategically placed clothing is far more arousing than simple nudity.

We rinsed and soaped off the dirt, blood and grime and though some of the women stayed up and hit the hot tub and the pool, Colby headed for bed and I jogged home in the moonlight. *Maybe everything will work out after all,* I thought as I finally slipped into my own bed at about two.

I slept until noon.

## 9

When I woke up, I felt a slight shiver of tension go through me as I realized I wasn't alone. I turned my head to see Will on the opposite side of the bed. I must have been seriously out of it to not remember him crawling under the sheets with me, but his presence calmed my fears.

He stared at me with a wicked grin on his face. "Tonight's the night," he began to sing. "For the sinners and the saints. When the worlds collide, in a beautiful display." He was singing Toby Mac, *City on our Knees* and I wondered at his choice, but I did love the song and he rarely sang. Will had been in choir with us at school, but he rarely sang out loud anymore. I guess he was self-conscious.

I closed my eyes and let him serenade me awake.

We spent the afternoon lounging around the pool. Elle had taken JR to the city while Amber and the Street Witches prepared for the ritual that evening. Adam had arrived with a bunch of hard-looking men and women in black SWAT gear, kissed my cheek hello, told me we'd catch up later, and went to set up a perimeter on Mt. Rettig. He said he was using motion sensors and his team was loaded up with tranq darts for batshit crazy werewolves or any other threat.

I hoped he wouldn't have to use them. The lycan-thropes, nonconformists that they were, were pooh-poohing the whole Blood Moon warning, but I wasn't so sure. It seems like tempting fate to even do it. Why not just skip the whole thing and everyone stay indoors? But in the end, they persuaded me to join in. It was hard to resist pack peer pressure, and wolves gotta howl, I guess.

Besides, Will wanted to get the party started with the pups, and I'd already agreed. If I was going to start acting more like a grownup, sticking to what I'd promised seemed like a good start. At least the pack had agreed not to go running all over the place, to stay in one area like we were camping, only with pelts and paws.

At sunset, we locked Colby in the cage as she insisted. Maybe the youngest of us was the only wise one. Then we went up to the crest of Mt. Rettig where at least a hundred witches surrounded the delegation while Master Shelby and his group of intimates presided.

This spell they had arranged was another layer of protection against the theoretical consequences of turning and mating during the Blood Moon. It was supposed to reroute any violent energies into the usual wolfish activities – running, hunting, playing, mating.

The whole thing seemed simple and innocuous except for the corpse flower, which they had to rub all over the shifters' foreheads. It attracted the most disgusting nocturnal zombie flies, but we endured.

The witches sang chants that sounded old as the heavens and finally ended with the incantation:

*Blood Moon fever*
*Fears abate*
*To escape thy violent fate*
*Sublimate, sublimate*
*Make werewolf love to thy chosen mate*

Well, that seemed unsubtle enough. Bring on the orgy? Or not, if that "chosen mate" line was supposed to ensure the wolves were monogamous tonight. I guess this was the compromise between lycanthrope laissez-faire and uptight witchiness.

When it was done, Amber and the witches disappeared off the mountain and the doggie delegation stripped and sat waiting. The moon rose and bled from orange to rust as the shadow of Earth crossed its face. It was a sight to behold, and the tension to shift built and built. I could tell this one was going to be different.

I just didn't know how different.

Normally I stayed conscious throughout the turning, but this time was reminiscent of the first time when I lost all control and most of the memories, so overwhelmed by the lunar energies was I. This time, I felt as if the moon were pouring its light into me, making me glow, filling me and my seven chakras with its primal essence.

That was the last thing I remembered until I awoke the next morning on the floor of our campsite, spooning with Will on my front side...and Jackson snuggled up to my back.

"Um, guys." I cleared my throat and elbowed Jackson in the gut.

He groaned. "A little bit lower and you would have gotten my nuts."

Will began to wake, so I stood and performed a quick leap over the men. Some women would have thought they'd died and gone to heaven. I just felt nauseated and proceeded to drive the point home as I retched, naked, over a fallen log.

"What's wrong with Ashlee?" Will asked.

"Must have been something she ate," Jackson dead-panned and loped over to join his human mate. Sully was already standing by a small camp stove set up on an old picnic table and was happily percolating coffee, old-school, in a battered steel pot. A stack of paper cups, cream and sugar waited beside it.

Jackson kissed Sully a good morning and asked, "Everyone accounted for?"

"As far as I can tell. Do you remember anything that happened last night?"

"Not a thing," Jackson said. "But my wolf is still asleep and satisfied. So, it can't have been that bad. No disasters, right?" He sniffed the air. "Do you smell...?"

"Colby, yeah," Sully answered. "I think we'd better check on the kid. You've got her cell phone, right?"

Jackson nodded and began to dress.

Colby, here? That couldn't be right. I mean, I'd left her locked in my cage. They must be mistaken. Maybe they smelled her on my clothes or something.

I'd finished tossing my cookies and turned to find Will handing me a cup of coffee for mouthwash, when I heard Ziggy barking in my head.

*Ashlee! You've got to get home now! Amber's in a coma and I can't reach her!* His voice came through loud and clear. In fact, it seemed the whole pack heard it. Must be a canine thing.

"Sounds like you'd best get home," Jackson said and pointed to the vehicles waiting for us at the trailhead.

Will and I shimmied into our clothes and raced for the parking lot, throwing ourselves into a car and telling the driver to step on it. Out the window I saw Adam standing in all his killer gear, finger to his ear, watching in puzzlement as we drove by.

I blew open the twin bond, but got nothing. Will called Samantha, while I phoned Adam to give him a quick, reassuring report and ask about last night.

"Yes, we did have an audible alarm go off and one of my men reported a wolf heading toward the interior of our perimeter, but I thought it must have been one of you guys getting too frisky, not a wolf coming in from outside."

"Some security you are."

"Hey, you try guarding a whole square mile of wooded mountains in the dark with twenty men. There's only so much I can do."

"Yeah, sorry. Thanks." I hung up. Then I called Con. Yes, I had the vampire on speed dial. I didn't like it, but this was my reality. As Bob Dylan once said, it may be the Devil or it may be the Lord, but you're gonna have to serve somebody, and Con had his place in things, even if he wasn't as much in charge as he liked to think.

Sister Lena, Ziggy and Colby met us at the door. I ran through the kitchen to my sister's bedroom. Nurse Sam was already hooking Amber up with an IV. Elle was looking lost holding her partner's hand.

Peg sat in a chair next to Elle, praying, and Con stood in a corner of the room. Even with the shades drawn he looked incredibly pale in the indirect day glow. I wondered how much sunlight he could tolerate before he burst into flames, or whatever vampires really did outside of movies.

Meanwhile, Ghost Mom floated like a worried angel above the lot of us.

"What happened?" I demanded.

"You happened," Elle said, and then she bit her lip.

Ouch. I began to cry. Maybe I deserved that. No matter how much good I did in the world, deep down, I always felt like a colossal screw-up.

Ziggy bumped me in the crotch and I dropped to the carpeted floor to hold him.

"Siegfried, come," Elle said, cruelly, I thought.

*I'm sorry, Ashlee,* he thought at me and he went to comfort his mistress, but Spanky was more than happy to take his place. At least one member of the family still loved me.

Peg was the one who acted the adult and jumped into the fray. "Don't let Elle blame you, Ash. Apparently Amber got up suddenly in the middle of the night and recited the ride-along spell. Elle thought she was dreaming, but she found Amber on the floor in a coma when she woke up this morning."

"So, where is she, Ziggy?" I asked. "Her spirit, I mean."

*I can't tell. She didn't jump into me,* the poodle said.

I told them, "Ziggy doesn't know and I've pinged the twin bond, but all I get is this echo in my head."

"She's traumatized," Ghost Mom said. Of course nobody else except for Ziggy and Spanky heard her.

"What do you mean, she's traumatized? I'm talking to Ghost Mom," I told the room.

"Amber had a premonition, woke up scared and apparently cobbled together a spell on the fly. I think she thought she was going to jump into your body, but the closest shifter in proximity was..."

"Colby," I said, jumping to the nearest conclusion. I quickly relayed the message and turned to find the teenager standing at the bedroom door, Sister Lena behind her.

"I think she's in my head," the kid said. "She's not saying much. But, when I close my eyes, I see her curled up in the dark in the fetal position. When my wolf tries to get close to comfort her, she just stares wide-eyed and whimpers."

"So what do we do?"

"Amber's like that monkey who shoved his hand into a coconut to get a trinket, but because he's got his hand bunched in a fist, he can't get it back out," Mom said and I repeated.

"So, what, I'm the coconut?" Colby asked.

I couldn't help but laugh. I'm sorry. I'm inappropriate that way. When things get awkward and dark, I get snarky. It's an involuntary defense. "In other words, whatever it is that's keeping her there…"

Mom finished for me. "She's gotta let it go."

"I guess we need to wait until she's ready to talk." I relayed that to the room while Elle got up and faced Colby down.

The girl tried to back away, but Sister Lena stood beside her whispering in her ear. "This isn't about you, Colby," she said to the frightened teenager. "Elle just needs you to be strong while she delivers a message to her wife."

"But…"

"You can do this. Remember, this isn't about you," Sister Lena said.

Before I knew what the hell was happening, Elle had taken Colby into her arms and laid a smackaroo on the young lycanthrope the likes of which I know I've never seen from the two of them – my sister-in-law and Amber, I mean. For a moment there, I felt a movement in the ethereal force. It was as if the twin bond thrummed within me. I placed a hand on my nervous stomach.

Then she, Elle, looked deep into the heart of the teenage werewolf, to where my sister's spirit might be lurking, and said, "Take all the time you need, love. That's just one of the things waiting for you when you return."

Instead of standing there with my mouth open looking shocked, I turned to Con and said, "You'll donate some of your magicky blood if we need you to, right?"

To which Peg answered, "Of course he will."

But Elle was having none of it. "All of you need to clear out. Colby, would you mind staying in the guest room so you can be close? Amber was going to offer it to you anyway while you were in town."

"Sure, no worries," Colby said, so we all left Elle to sit with Amber's body.

We seemed to be at somewhat of a collective loss, and stood around making uneasy small talk. Will suggested we fix breakfast, so we threw out a spread my sister would have been proud of. It only dawned on me a little later that, when Colby began to pitch in, it was like she had a sense of where everything was, despite never having been there. Not once did I tell her where to find anything. And if that didn't convince me that my twin sister was still alive in the young were, I don't know what would.

It took Amber a couple of days to come out of her spiritual catatonia, during which time there were *way* too many people traipsing in and out of the Gordon-Scott house than was normal and to my sister's liking, what with witches and werewolves and all. I think it might have been that more than anything as I saw Colby's eyes narrow at the coffee rings on the kitchen counters, spurring Amber toward recovery. Never underestimate the primal rage of an OCD housekeeper.

We weres still couldn't remember most of the details about what happened over the Blood Moon, but I was getting disturbing flashes from my wolf, coming clearer all the time.

I called Adam and tried to get more information, but he told me his people had merely manned the perimeter and made sure the wolves stayed within bounds. He repeated the report about when the perimeter alarms had been triggered, but to him it had seemed one of the younger wolves had wandered too close to the demarcation zone.

That reminded me about Jackson and Sully claiming to smell Colby. Hmm. I'd have to dig further into this.

Later, according to Adam, what he saw from the high-powered binoculars he was using, we all took down a longhorn steer and there seemed to be a lot of wolf-sex going on, and then we all laid down and fell asleep. He'd let his team go once he started to see signs of morning and confirmed all the sleepers looked human again. After everyone had awoken, he'd left as well.

Colby pulled me aside one morning as we were sitting at the main house kitchen peninsula chowing down on donuts from Crave. "Amber wants to talk to you."

"Oh, thank God!" I answered. I'd felt the twin bond twitching, but the emotion and turmoil I was getting, without any clarity of information to back it up, was seriously chapping my hide.

"Alone," she said, lowering her voice, so I grabbed a few Bavarian crèmes and a couple of coffees and we exited the main house, rounded the pool and entered my domain.

"I don't drink coffee," Colby said.

"But Amber does," I told her.

She smiled my sister's smile, which was hella weird coming from someone else, and took a sip before setting it on the coffee table, along with the pastries.

We sat cross-legged on the futon, facing each other. "So, how does this work?" I asked.

"Amber can take control of my body if I let her. All I have to do is step aside in my own head and her consciousness comes forward. But you should know, I do hear and see everything, so whatever Amber tells you, I'll end up knowing."

"Yeah, I got that part. Well, Colby, little sister, guess it's time for some TMI." I was making light of the situation, but deep down I was seriously worried.

Colby closed her eyes and relaxed, breathing deeply. When she opened them and looked at me, I realized that it was Amber behind those orbs.

"Oh Amb," I said and moved forward to cradle her in my arms. She let me for a moment, then sniffled and pushed me back.

"Don't make me cry, Ashlee," she said, then bogarted one of my donuts and began to eat. "Oh my God, this is *soo* good," she said.

My jaw dropped. My sister was fastidious about what she ate, avoiding anything unhealthy.

"Don't look at me like that. The kid's young and she's a werewolf. Hell, in this body, I can eat whatever I want and she'll just burn it off. Beats being in Siegfried; I stay too long inside him and I'll be begging Elle for table scraps."

"So, what happened?"

She finished the sugary confection, very messily, and then used the hand sanitizer she always carried with her no matter what body she seemed to be inhabiting.

Then, with Colby's mouth, Amber shared.

"After the Street Witches did the Blood Moon protection spell we were all pretty wiped, so I went to bed early. I heard a strange noise out back, and I woke up absolutely terrified for you, Ash. I shouldn't have, I guess, but I said the ride-along spell to try to jump to you and warn you, and the next thing I knew, I was in Colby and I was a wolf and tearing up the mountain following the sound of a whole lot of howling. I tried to stop my headlong rush to wherever I was, and then I thought to open up the twin bond, but you just weren't there. You must have already turned.

"Then it was like the pull of the moon and the need to run took Colby-wolf over, and dragged me along with it. It felt like that time I was riding horseback and I lost control of the horse. All I could do was hang on for dear life.

"Colby's wolf was so happy to be reunited with the pack, and at first, it was amazing. All of these alphas on display, primping and preening, sparring and dancing, playing tug-of-war with a beef carcass and eventually playing with each other. But something about Colby being there set everyone on edge."

"She's an unattached alpha female in her prime. I bet there was confusion." I said. "Without their human minds, they didn't know where to put her in the pecking order."

"Yes, well. I tried to steer her away from the males who looked like they were ready to mount her and the females who wanted to drive her off, but before I could, I saw something. Something awful."

"What was it?" I asked, dreading the answer.

"You were the other anomaly. Your wolf, I mean. I don't know how to tell you this, Ashlee, but your wolf isn't monogamous."

"I most certainly am," I said. "Wolves mate for life."

"Just let me tell it. While the rest of the pack was eating and the mated pairs were, um, doing it, you and Will were getting it on too."

"Getting it on. Nice image, Amb," I said, and turned my attention inward to my wolf, who'd been sitting up on her haunches, listening. She arched her head at me coyly, lay down belly up and showed me the little bulge we had going.

"So much for waiting. Guess Will got his wish after all," I said.

"I stayed upwind and watched your pack go from deadly predators to doggie style within a half hour. It was like having a front row seat to a National Geographic documentary."

I snorted. "Like that song – something about doing it like they do on the Discovery Channel?"

"Exactly. But your wolf, Ashlee – your wolf couldn't seem to stay still. After you and Will, you know, got done and he fell asleep – well, your wolf got up and decided to go for round two."

"Shit." I said and rubbed my belly. "Who was it?"

"Jackson. He was the only other unattached alpha male."

"Holy Mary Mother of God." What was I supposed to do with this information? My wolf didn't feel guilty about it; she looked pleased as punch. The human side of me, though, was...confused? Revolted? I wasn't at all sure, so I grabbed another donut and stuffed it into my face. Always a good response to stress, right?

"I was mortified, Ashlee. It was like a train wreck and I couldn't look away. I felt like washing out my eyeballs. There are some things a sister just shouldn't see. But that's not the worst part of it. Before you joined with Jackson, you turned," she said. "You turned *hybrid*, Ashlee. You weren't just lycanthrope and lupine, you did it as werewolves. Anubis form, I think you called it. Wolf-man to wolf-woman. It was *freaky*."

"Christ Almighty," I swore. *Forgive me God,* I thought. The Good Book says all things work together for good, but this may be pushing it. "I've never turned hybrid. I've seen Jackson do it, but I thought it was something that only alphas did."

"You're an alpha, Ashlee. Everyone in our natural family is. You, Adam, me, Dad, we all are."

*With great power comes great responsibility, my padawan,* Ziggy said into our heads.

What, poodles watch Star Wars? Like weirder things weren't happening.

"So, what does that mean for my…?" I rubbed my human belly in wolfish sympathy, afraid of any answer, which was a moot point because I don't think anyone had any idea anyway.

"I have no idea, but if I were you, I might consider termination."

"What? First, you berate me for not having enough maternal instincts, and then you advise me to abort." I said it in a rising snarl.

"We don't have to make the decision now," Amber said in that twin-sister-knows-best tone, "but it better be soon. From what I hear, the wolf's term is less than half of a humans."

My wolf snarled inside of me and I felt her claws rake across my soul. *Mine!* She howled in fear and anger and covered herself in darkness, leaving me alone in my head.

She didn't have to worry. No way was I going to do any harm to our children. "So, is that everything, or is there more?" I said it sarcastically, not expecting anything worse than this.

"Yes, actually –"

And then she shuddered and said, "Isn't that enough?" and I looked up to find my twin sister gone from Colby's eyes.

"What was Amber going to say?"

Colby's face turned cold. "Nothing that was her business to see. It was totally uncool to ride along like that without my permission. I tried to be nice about it and you needed to hear about what happened to you, but you don't need the details on what happened to me."

"What happened to you?" Then it hit me. She was rubbing her belly too, as if unaware she was doing it. "Who?"

She dropped her eyes. "Jackson. As it should be. We're fated to be mated. It wasn't supposed to happen so soon, but...it wasn't so bad."

*Amber's awake!* Ziggy called.

Colby leaped up to run to the main house and gather with the others at my sister's bedside. I let her go. I could tell with the twin bond that Amber was fine, physically anyway, and she had plenty of people to fuss over her. I locked my door, and then ran a hot bath to give myself time to think.

Eventually I called Will, told him Amber was all right and advised him not to come over, that I was taking some time to myself after all the stress we'd all been under. After that I crawled into bed and disappeared under the covers. I already had a lot on my plate and the heap of stink Amber just hit me with was much too much, doing it with two guys on one night. Pardon my French, but as far as I was concerned, the world could go fuck itself and I'd show back up when I was good and ready.

I spent the next few days in bed. Pre-partum depression is how I described it, or maybe it was post-impregnation. I mean, what do you do when you feel like your body isn't your own, and that it could get up and dance by itself and there wasn't anything you could do to stop it? Okay, only during the full moon, maybe only during freaking Blood Moons and then only with pack magic driving all the wolves into joyful frenzies.

I trudged around the house in my bathrobe. Stopped answering calls. Begged off my freelance assignments until I started to see the money run out of my account. And I pondered the state of the world and how I had come to this.

In retrospect, the whole thing seemed stupider and stupider. Why hadn't we all just locked ourselves in and suffered through a night in solitary confinement? Yeah, the witches had cast their spell of protection, but maybe they'd only made things worse. In fact, maybe they'd caused the whole thing! It was like that Oracle chick in the Matrix had said, something about what was cause and what was effect when prophecies came into play.

In other words, what if the predicted disaster was caused by the very spell of sublimation that turned our bloodlust into, well, just *lust?* What if that was what the warning was about, and we'd walked straight into it?

After thinking some more, though, I wondered if I was again the main object of someone's machinations. So, tell me, how do you turn a victim into a hero? I kept thinking I'd wake up and have some idea.

I logged into Facebook and followed the highlight reels of some former friends' lives. I finally had to log off when I realized that it was making me feel like shit, seeing all their happy faces and their perfect families and their suburban lawns.

After a while I took a few homeopathic sleeping pills and tried to dream through it, thinking maybe my subconscious would give me some answers. Maybe I'd wake up later and things would look different. But the laters kept coming and the world still stayed the same.

Through it all I ignored my calls and only came up for air to tell Ziggy to tell Amber to tell everyone that I was fine, that I just didn't want to see anyone.

Aw, who was I kidding? Damned if I do, damned if I don't. No matter which way around it, I had been thoroughly screwed, by two guys, and who knows what the result would be? And should I tell Will, or should I keep this a secret? With Will in his current state of alpha-maleness, he would probably go after Jackson and get himself killed, or badly hurt anyway. Will might be my alpha, but he wasn't the pack's alpha.

No, I couldn't tell him. If he found out later, so be it. At least there would be a cushion of time in between. And as for me and my ambivalence? Best thing to do is accept the situation and move on, I told myself.

*Easier said than done, isn't it?* This from the Ziggy-Amber peanut gallery.

A wise woman once told me, "Happiness isn't about having what you want; it's about wanting what you have."

Was that my problem? I thought I knew what I wanted. But what if a person wanted changes? Then what?

Ugh. I slept again.

You know they say in therapy that it's not what happens to you in life that counts as much as how you respond to it. And speaking of therapy, do they even have

therapists for supernaturals? I'd have to ask Con about
that. Or Sully. I wasn't talking to Jackson until I had
a better handle on what I was going through and I had a
feeling that bending Ghost Mom's ear wasn't going to be
enough.

Whom could I talk to that I could trust? Amber had
made it perfectly clear what she thought, so she wasn't an
option. Ziggy was, well, a dog, Elle's dog and Amber's
familiar. Too close. I didn't know any of the witches well
enough, nor Will's sister Sam. Not for this.

Then I realized: I'd talk to Adam. Of all my family,
Adam seemed to be the rock we could always turn
to when we needed someone to have our backs, if rocks
had backs.

So I called Adam and told him the whole story. He
stopped me when we got to Amber's part. "So, how did
Colby get out anyway?"

"Wait, what?"

"You said that Amber woke up in Colby's body already
headed up the hill. I thought you said she was locked up.
Obviously she was the anomaly we had over in sector
eight. She must have come through and we were looking
for wolves going *out*, not coming in. Anyway, she was
supposed to be locked down, so we didn't suspect."

I could tell he was blaming himself. "She was. I locked
her in myself, but I didn't think about that until just now."

"Someone else must have sneaked in and let her out.
I'll send one of my people in to do a forensic sweep. Have
you been down in the basement since?"

"Only to do laundry. The bedding in the cage looked clawed up, but I wasn't even thinking about how Colby got out, what with Amber in a coma, and all. Oh, Adam, I feel so stupid," I said. "Not to mention violated."

"I'll talk to Elle about upgrading the property sensors and getting you on a dedicated line. You might want to have a witch you trust come in and do a magical sweep."

"Wait, you think the witches are involved?"

"I wouldn't put it past them. Why?"

"It's just, they've been all over the place while Amber was in her coma. You don't think one of them…"

"I don't know, Ashlee. Better safe than sorry. Are there any of the witches you would specifically trust or distrust?"

"Naw, they're all kooky and weird, but nobody stands out as especially unnerving. Sister Lena seems to have a good head on her shoulders."

"She's leader of the coven," Adam said. "I'll send her in to do a broom-sweep."

"A broom-sweep?"

"What did you think witches' brooms were for? Flying?"

"Umm…"

"Do you know how much magical power it takes to levitate? Don't believe everything you read. It's like we do it for bugs, only for magic. Anyway, tell me what happened after Amber woke up playing sidecar to Colby's wolf."

I continued the story without interruption until the end. "So, what do you think I should do?"

"Sounds like you've already made up your mind."

"Gee, thanks."

"I would have told you to ride it out anyway. I mean, it's not like you were raped or like they have birth defects, right? I'm not that parental myself and I know it's not politically correct, a woman's body and all, but I still think you should carry the pups to term."

"You would. You started all this, anyway." After all, he'd sent the werewolves to my door in the first place, though I didn't have to open it.

"I did?" His voice got all innocent-like.

"Some day you're going to sit down and tell me everything you know about Knightsbridge, supernaturals and just what you do in that top secret job of yours."

"I am, eh?" He laughed. "Believe me, Ash, you're better off not knowing. But my main job right now is to keep my sisters safe, with Dad and Rhonda none the wiser."

"Speaking of which, you may want to make plans with Dad over Halloween, as Rhonda's coming to Knightsbridge for the Street Witches Convention."

"Why?"

"I guess she's getting into witchcraft. Or was already."

"Really? Wonder if Dad knows he's in an interfaith marriage. Didn't see that one coming."

"I know, right?" My neck was getting stiff from cradling the phone on my shoulder and I groaned. "Take him to a movie. I bet it's been a while since he's been in a real theater. He's such a bookworm."

"Roger wilco," he said. "Oh, and remember, expect a visit from my forensics guy. I'd like to know *who let the dogs out*."

"Who, who?" I groaned at his punishment. I bet he was waiting the whole conversation just to slide that one past me, but that's my brother: deadly, with a juvenile sense of humor.

"By Ashface."

"By, Alien," I said and hung up. I always felt better after talking to Adam. It's not like my situation had changed or anything; he just made me feel less alone in the midst of it.

A guy named Nick showed up the next morning with an actual CSI kit. Two, really, one in each hand, opening like tackle boxes with their stairstep holders. Fingerprint powder. Tape. Beakers and eyedroppers and cotton swabs and solutions, plastic zip-lock bags and rubber gloves and more obscure whatnots.

And he was deadly cute. Good thing I was already *soo* monogamous. Then my wolf derailed that thought and I felt bad all over again.

"Whoever set Colby free did a good job of covering his tracks," Nick said after testing around the linoleum and the bars of the cage. He crawled in and squatted on his gloved hands and padded knees and surveyed the mass of thrashed bedding. He rifled through the scraps, grabbed something and turned to me and held out his hand. "Isn't this one of your scarves?"

It was one of the scarves I'd given to the Delegation of Bitches. In fact, it was the scarf I'd given to Sierra. I knew because it was the ugliest of the lot. Maybe it was petty of me to give her the one I liked the least, but she didn't have to know it. One man's trash is another man's treasure and all that.

"Sierra," I said.

Nick said, "But she was up on the mountain with us during the change, right? Even if she was involved, she couldn't have done it herself. Nobody got out."

I shrugged. "Maybe it's a setup. Everyone knows I hate Sierra. Adam's sending a witch in to check for magical traces. Said if you don't find anything, Sister Lena's the best next bet."

Someone knocked on the door upstairs. "Speak of the devil," I said and headed up to let the witch in.

Sister Lena entered with a swiffer and a dustpan, followed by Spanky, Ziggy, Ghost Mom, Colby and Amber, in that order. Hoo boy.

"We invited Elle too," Colby said as if reading my thoughts, "but she seemed more interested in the game."

"Small mercies." I looked to my sister and we smiled. Gotta love Elle. Our island of normal in a sea of insanity. I was glad she seemed to have forgiven me now that Amber was normal again. At least as normal as she ever is. "A swiffer?"

"Hey, we're modern when we can be," Lena said.

Nick came up from the basement and gave us the all-clear; forensically, that is. "I'll take what I got to the lab and see what I can figure out." Then he left.

Sister Lena said, "I hope you don't mind, Ashlee, but when Adam called and said you needed a broom-sweep, Siegfried and I decided that this would make a good teaching opportunity for Amber's training."

"And the rest of you?" I looked at the others.

*Oh, we're just here for moral support,* Ziggy thought at us, and we all had to laugh.

"Well, this I gotta see," I said. Hey, if my space was going to be invaded, I might as well be entertained.

"All right, Amber. You know what to do," Sister Lena said and I watched as my sister lit a bundle of sage in a conch shell and proceeded to fan the fumes into every corner of my open studio layout. She then proceeded down into the basement and eventually even crawled her way up the tunnel to the duck blind.

I watched as she crouched low and returned, dirt smudges on her elbows and knees. I expected her to bitch and moan about how filthy I kept my escape hatch, but she didn't say a word. When she got back to the main floor, she chanted for a moment, centered herself, and then held the dustpan in one hand and the swiffer in the other.

*Magic broom*
*Within this keep*
*Magic broom*
*This house to sweep*
*Gather up the charms and bugs*
*Reveal the spies, the thieves and thugs*
*Show us spells they may have placed*
*Repeat the paths that they have traced*
*Sweep this place from top to bottom*
*Cleanse this space from all things rotten!*

My twin tossed the cleaning tools into the air, and I kid you not, those things began to dance. Up across the cathedral ceiling that housed the kitchen and dining room they slid past walls and windows, over crossbeams and light fixtures, and even zipped down to the blades of the ceiling fan. Each place they went, the dustpan caught whatever the modern-day-broomy thing swept.

I was afraid that the pan would get weighed down by the leavings of my poor housekeeping skills. I think Amber worried too as she narrowed her eyes and pulled her shirt up over her nose and mouth against the dust.

But the dust kept disappearing and every now and then I saw something sparkle in the pan. When the swiffer found the basement stairs, we all followed, but it was a bit anticlimactic, just more of the same, until it finally stopped in the middle of the tile floor.

Amber picked up the broom and dustpan and we returned to the living room where Amber emptied the sparkling dust into a Tibetan singing bowl I'd gotten in India. Bet no one ever used it for this before. My eyes began to water and I had to escape outside for a momentary allergy attack.

When I returned, Amber had surrounded the singing bowl with crystals. She rubbed her hands together as if to generate heat, and then placed her hands over the opening.

*Secrets and stories to tell*
*Make this bowl a wishing well*
*Show us now what's trapped within*
*The face of he or she who sinned*

And I swear, when she lifted her hands, the air above the bowl shimmered. It was like that hologram of Princess

Leah, only this showed my basement and Colby the wolf locked in the cage.

The scene shifted and we saw a dark, hooded figure enter the pool house and slip down the stairs. Colby turned and became agitated at the presence of the stranger. The cloaked one pointed and the lock snapped open and fell off the cage. He sent a ball of light probing and it bounced off the trigger tile for the escape tunnel and opened the way out. Then he took both hands and, in a sweeping gesture, sent a cloud of sparkles that pushed Colby's wolf out of the basement and up the tunnel to the duck blind.

He then took the scarf I'd given Sierra out of his pocket, shook it out and threw it into the cage.

"I *knew* it wasn't Sierra," I muttered.

The rest of the group shushed me.

What? I figured we'd seen all the pertinent details, unless we got a look at the guy. At least I assumed it was a guy from his build and the way he moved. As sneaky as he was being, we probably wouldn't get a decent look at him before he left.

And then, wiping his hands like Pontius Pilate, the man doffed his hood and turned full frontal to our perspective. Don't ask me how magic chooses its angle.

Amber and I gasped. It was Willoughby, the street preacher from the night we'd all gone cruising. And then the figure blazed and disappeared, but before it did, in the midst of the brightness, staring right at us, was an evil face with piercing eyes and a laughing sneer, a face I was sure I knew.

"Whoa, who was that?" Colby asked. "'Cause she is one scary –"

"– bitch!" Amber and I both spoke at once.

"Jeanetta Macdonald," I followed up. "I thought you witches were supposed to be keeping her under control!"

Sister Lena shot me a look. "There's only so much we can do. At least now we know. I don't think we were supposed to see that last part. We were supposed to think it was that poor deluded man. You did a very good job, Amber. I've got to make a phone call." She went outside, followed by Colby and Spanky.

I turned to Amber and snarled, "I should have killed her when I had the chance."

*Stop it Ashlee. You know you're not a murderer.*

*Preemptive self-defense,* I thought back at her.

*I know some people,* Ziggy offered.

Amber and I rounded on him and spoke as one. "No!"

He looked miffed, stuck his nose up into the air and exited to the backyard, there to do his business in the middle of the lawn.

And he says he's not really a dog.

Sister Lena soon returned, followed by Elle, who had been outside sitting on the divan on the patio, watching baseball. Colby stood inside the threshold, leaning against the doorframe.

"Jeanetta's been in a coma for a week now," Lena pronounced.

"So, just before the Blood Moon," Amber said.

"She must have done a ride-along spell," I finished my sister's thought. "It's the only answer."

"Or worse," said Lena. "Full possession of a mortal."

"You people can do that?" I spat. Okay, I was taking a swig from a bottle of water at the time, so that was my excuse.

"*You people*, Ash?" my twin retorted. "Nice."

"Sorry." At least I had the decency to feel embarrassed. Life was easier when it was us and them.

"We need to find Willoughby." Amber turned to Elle. "Can you?"

"I already know what happened to him." Elle crossed her arms over her chest. "He's dead. They found him in a dumpster behind the Boxcar."

"I didn't see that in the papers," I said.

"Let's just say his death had suspicious undertones," Elle replied. "The mayor's keeping the police investigation under wraps. Con's looking into it, too."

"Why weren't we informed?" Sister Lena asked.

"He had a pentagram carved into his chest?" Amber cried. Through the twin bond, I caught her picking the image from Elle's brain.

"Don't do that," Elle said.

"Sorry." She didn't sound sorry.

Upright or inverted? I froze the image in my mind and examined it. Two points upward, I decided. An inverted pentagram evoked the image of the goat, the horned one, the devil, and stood for bad juju no matter how you sliced it.

"We didn't know who could be involved." Elle said.

"Well, now we do," I told her. "But why kill her ride-along?"

"The longer Jeanetta's away from her body, the more power she needs to sustain the spell," Sister Lena said. "She's using blood magick. Another prisoner was murdered just before she fell into the coma."

"So, what we can expect? More innocent bodies to pop up?" I said.

*What's a guilty body?* Ziggy sniped from across the lawn.

*You know what I mean, silly daemon.*

"How long can she possess someone before she needs to take another victim?" Elle asked, getting to the heart of the matter.

"The longest I've heard of someone doing a ride-along is a couple of weeks. If she's doing a full possession, she can do a week tops before she has to kill again to power the spell. Otherwise the prime personality will kick her out."

"So, what you're saying is that you really don't know," Elle countered, disapproval showing on her face.

"Witchcraft is not an exact science," Sister Lena huffed.

"So, how do we find her and nullify this threat, once and for all?" I asked.

"And how do we get this bitch out of our lives?" Amber and Elle said together. I know, right? Spooky.

"What if her body dies while she's riding someone else?" Colby asked. Leave it to kids to think outside the box. Or outside the body, in this case.

"That's not an option," Sister Lena said, and swept regally out the door.

*Not to you, maybe,* I thought. Guess I needed to have another chat with Con, and maybe Adam too. They wouldn't have any problem taking care of business.

Oh hell, it looked like it was time for another come-to-Jesus-and-Satan meeting. Hope they don't end up killing the messenger, AKA *me.*

Sigh.

## 10

My stomach was in knots all day. Amber had been bugging me about the pregnancy and it took all my deep-breathing exercises not to tell her to go take a long walk off a short pier.

"Ashlee, you need to be responsible about this. You have no idea what metaphysical door you've opened."

"I'm *not* aborting my pups," I told her and slammed the twin bond closed for emphasis.

She looked down her nose at me and said, "Well, then at least do the next smartest thing and talk about this with Jackson and Will."

"Jackson, maybe. Chances are I'm not going to get judgment from that sector for something I had no decision in anyway, but Will? Why should I tell him? It would probably send him over the edge. I mean, I know that I'm the gal that rips the band-aid off, but not everybody actually wants that."

I'd been having this argument in my head since I'd found out, and surprisingly enough it felt good to get it out in the open.

Amber said, "Let's plot this out like you were writing a piece, a story. What if you don't tell him? Either of them?

You have no idea what you're going to actually give birth to. What happens if your wolf goes into labor and you need assistance with the birth? Who's going to be around to save you if you run into trouble, much less a litter of puppies?"

"Oh." I hadn't thought of that. Hadn't thought of anything past, *omigod, I'm gonna be a mommy-wolf!*

"You seem incredibly calm considering the ramifications of your actions."

"I don't know, Amber. I guess I'm resigned to it, and my wolf, which is half of me anyway, is ecstatic. The actual experience of my wolf having puppies doesn't worry me. I'm more freaked out about how Will is going to look at me after I tell him. I have to believe that the Divine Eternal has a plan for all of this."

"Pulling the spirituality card, eh?" she said.

"At the end of the day, when life gives you shit just for trying to be a decent person, trying to love your neighbor as yourself and all that, what else do we have?"

"We all must answer to our Maker," she finished for me.

And as much as it pained me to do so, I knew I was going to have to tell both Jackson and Will the truth. What's that saying? It takes a village?

I just hoped I wouldn't turn into the village leper.

***

I heard what happened later, but I'll tell it to you now as if I were watching:

My mate Will Stenfield stood at the glass counter in Knightsbridge Canyon Jewelry Exchange holding the small velvet box with his mom's engagement ring. He'd had it refitted for Ashlee and he was planning to pop the question. He heard a commotion behind him and turned.

"Why Will Stenfield? What do you have there?" An unfamiliar face peered back at him.

"I'm sorry. Do I know you?"

"Layolin Potter. Abbess Layolin, to my friends. I'm a friend of Amber's. We're working on the Street Witches Convention together. She showed me your picture." The woman beamed, stuck out her hand to shake and pumped his free one enthusiastically. "You're much handsomer in real life, I have to say."

"Thanks, I think," he countered deadpan and rescued his hand from her impressive grip.

"It looks like I caught you deep in thought. Anything you'd like to share?" she asked, nodding pointedly to the jewelry box.

"No. I'm fine, really," Will said, pocketing the item. "Just woolgathering. And if you know Ash, I'd appreciate you not mentioning that you saw me here, it being for a surprise and all, you understand."

"Curiouser and curiouser," Abbess Layolin teased. "Well, whatever it is you've got on your mind, I do hope you get the result you're hoping for. Mum's the word." She brushed her hand down his arm, causing the hair on his skin to rise as if by static electricity.

He felt a jolt in his brain and grabbed her arm, small claws beginning to extend from his fingers. All manner of kindness vanished from the witch's eyes and she glared at him with hatred like he'd never seen.

Through gritted teeth, she smiled, and said, "Take your hand off my arm unless you want to draw back a stump. Oh, and tell Ashlee I'm coming for her."

He let her go and she fell to the floor, writhing like an epileptic having a seizure.

A sales clerk ran over. "What happened?"

"I don't know," Will replied, as he cradled the crazy witch's head. He'd gotten his wolf back under control, but even touching this woman was giving him the heebie-jeebies. "Call 911."

I found out about all of that the same night at a meeting called by Con up at the ranch house – minus the bit about the jewelry box, of course. And after what I had to tell him, who could blame Will for holding that little tidbit back. What you don't know can't hurt you, right?

Don't answer that.

We all sat around the ranch house dining room table in a formal meeting: Constantine Shelby, Master of Knightsbridge, Jackson and Sully as pack-masters; Sister Lena and Sister Nayala as representative of the witches; my brother Adam, and Will and me.

"And the weird thing is," Will finished. "When she sent that probe of dark magick or whatever it was into me, I didn't see Abbess Potter's face anymore. I saw Jeanetta Macdonald."

"Jesus, Mary and Joseph!" Sister Lena erupted.

The irony got me, so of course I snickered. Okay, I snorted. Are you happy now? I know, I know, were-pig, that's me.

Sister Lena continued, "I don't know how she managed to infiltrate the inner circle. But that explains why Abbess Layolin is in a coma. I hope we can find a thread of her astral form and call it back from wherever it went when Jeanetta took over. Usually the trauma from the violation of possession sends the main personality into hiding, gathering resources to return and overthrow the possessor."

"You know, I hate to have to rely on it," Adam interrupted. "But I'm thinking we need some extra magical protection for Amber and Ash. Sister Lena, can you have the witches ward the grounds? Maybe something like an invitation-only spell?"

"What would that look like?" Sister Nayala turned to Adam and he beamed back at her. Did my brother have a bit of a crush? Mental note to ask him later.

"Just like how vampires can't enter a private residence without being invited. Can't we extend the same mojo to all supernaturals? I got the humans covered, but maybe all magical beings have to be invited past the threshold as well."

"Well, that would protect them while on the property, but we should get them some mobile protection also," Sister Lena said.

"I could whip up some charms that will protect them from psychic intrusion," Sister Nayala mused. "Maybe magical dog collars for when the pack is turned."

"Make sure you make mine large enough, with rainbow sparkles. And Sully would prefer a hot pink with spangles," Jackson deadpanned.

"Are you sure this isn't a bit of overkill?" Con asked.

I narrowed my eyes at him. I think he was afraid he was going to lose his tenuous hold over the werewolves as his servants to call.

"Better safe than sorry, vampire," my brother said, and Con shrugged, picking an imaginary something out of his perfect fingernails.

"Do you have any better ideas?" I asked, willing to give Con the benefit of the doubt.

"We could just kill Jeanetta in prison where she sleeps." He looked at the skeptical faces and amended, "Or we could give her a partial lobotomy. Throw some electrodes on her, kill a few brain cells. Or a long needle up the nostril would..." he trailed off at the looks of horror on our faces.

"You are seriously beginning to worry me," I told Con. "Why do your solutions always involve hurting people?"

"We're monsters, Ashlee," Con replied.

"Speak for yourself," I muttered.

"Don't deny you thought of it yourself."

I didn't deny it, because I had. "I rejected outright murder and hoped you'd have a better idea."

He put a finger to his temple. "I'm still up for lobotomy."

"Moving on." Damn, if I didn't sound just like Amber there for a moment.

"Then again, the witches could just do a binding spell," he said reasonably. "A permanent one."

So, that was his game. Lead with crazy and follow up with sensible. I mean, John the Baptist helped make Jesus look acceptable. Malcolm X did the same thing for Martin Luther King.

Then again, look what happened to *those* two.

"You have no idea what you're asking, fang," Sister Lena looked affronted.

"Why? Can you do it? Bind her magic permanently?" I said, remembering the scene in *The Craft* where Robin Tunney tries to bind Fairuza Balk when her lust for power got out of hand.

"Having your powers bound is one of the most isolating things you can do to a witch. With the drugs, at least she can still sense the elements even if she can't influence or command them. To bind a witch is like crippling a child so he won't ever run away. We only do it as a last resort," Sister Lena explained. "Imagine if someone took away your sense of smell, Ashlee. All of a sudden the world wouldn't make sense anymore. Most bound witches take their lives if we let them, or they end up in mental hospitals. If a witch doesn't want to rehabilitate, you get someone like Jeanetta Macdonald. Believe it or not, the drugs we use, herbal remedies, are more humane. Antidepressant drugs can have the same effect."

"Which would explain why the streets aren't covered with witches, as many of their powers are suppressed," Sister Nayala added. "I did my graduate work on the effects of dopamine and serotonin on a witch's magical disposition."

Adam seemed entranced, and Sister Nayala beamed back at him. The level of arousal in the room went up a notch and I growled at him.

Adam winked at me. "I think we've got this covered." He rose as if to leave. "Ashlee?" he held out his hand as if beckoning me to come with him. My brother, the Knight Errant. "Nayala, would you like a ride back home after I drop off Ash?"

I noted his dropping the title "Sister." Sister Nayala had come with Lena, but my brother was offering her a ride. I hoped she wouldn't be just another of his conquests. Did Templars take vows of celibacy? I didn't actually know.

"I need to stay and talk to Jackson and Will," I told him.

Once Adam and Nayala had left, I turned to the guys. "Take a walk?"

Reluctantly, as if they knew something bad was coming, they followed me.

I walked past the corral. The horses were all in the barn bedded down for the night and we climbed up onto the rails of the corral, hooked our feet in the slats and stared up at the waning moon.

"So, I bet you've wondered why I've called you all here tonight."

"Christ, Ashlee. Just get it over with," Will said. "I can you feel you vibrating with tension all through the fenceposts."

"Please don't take the Lord's name in vain," I said, not so much defending my intermittent faith as taking the cheap out by being a petty bitch.

Jackson cut that argument off at the pass. "I assume this is about what happened during the Blood Moon."

"So, what do you remember?" I asked Jackson.

"More than you, I suspect. Why don't you tell me what you know and I'll fill in the details."

"What are you two talking about? I can't remember a thing," Will said.

*Oh joy*, I thought. *Here goes nothing.*

I told them about the street preacher's invasion of my home. I told them about Colby trying to join us during the Blood Moon orgy. I told them how Amber rode Colby and watched what happened. How Will and I mated, and how Jackson and I...

You know.

I didn't even have to look at him to know that tears were filling Will's eyes. I could feel the vibration of his rage, and anger, and impotence.

Will hopped off the fence. Jackson followed.

"Um, Jackson," I began, meaning to beg him off. Will always needed alone time to process things, but eventually he came back around.

I hoped. I prayed. Lord, don't let it be this time that pushes him away.

"This is men's business, Ashlee. Stay and watch if you must, but don't say a word and for the love of the moon, don't interfere," Jackson said.

For once, I did as I was told.

Will sank to his knees and began to howl, and I sensed the beginning of the shift.

Jackson joined him, cradling the smaller man as both raised their faces to the sky.

As one they grappled, rising from their knees as if locked in combat. Arms rippled with muscle and fur, clothes split at chest, calf and thigh. Their claws lengthened as they held tight to each other, blood welling from the wounds until finally Will kicked his legs into Jackson's stomach and they broke away.

The hybrid Anubis form was frightening on the least of lycanthropes, but these two huge males were positively terrifying. I couldn't imagine interfering. You can say *rah-rah, girl power* all you want, but when it came to a physical contest, well…this was what nature designed males for: vicious fighting, win or die.

On a good day, such brutality worked to protect the pack. On a bad day, it turned against itself. To be honest, I wasn't sure what kind of a day this was at all.

Like gladiators in the arena, they circled each other. A feint here, a touch there, they paced out a round and wove back and forth, looking for an opening. Moving forward to kick and slash, one scoring here, one scoring there. So fast, the wounds seemed to appear as if by magic, healing soon after.

Blood spurted on Jackson from a roundhouse to the jaw and I cheered Will on. I couldn't help it. Then Jackson ripped a gash in Will's thigh and I groaned.

Bruises and wounds came and went in the wake of the lycanthropic magic. I was spellbound and exhausted just watching the two of them. For fully half an hour they went at it, cleaving each other with their pain and anguish at the situation I'd put them in.

I don't know why what happened next came as a surprise to me, but it did. Ghost Mom sat down next to me and I felt her marshmallow softness and inhaled her scent. *They both love you very much.*

They both loved me. In different ways, of course, and with different privileges and expressions, but I belonged to them. They both had hold of my heart. And I realized, this wasn't a fight for dominance I was watching. It was two alpha males bleeding out the violence within themselves, clearing the way for a new version of family.

It was a battle for respect from each other, a battle that needed no winner.

It was a battle for love.

When the men were finally spent and their Anubis forms slipped away, Jackson held Will in his arms as if he were his son instead of his rival, memorizing his scent and helping him become one with his pack once again. The older male cocked his head as if just now noticing me and beckoned with his hand.

Ghost Mom gave me a push and I stumbled forward off the railing I'd been sitting on, not sure what to expect. Until then I'd never been privileged to bear witness to such a powerful display of raw male passion and gentility.

Luckily, my wolf knew what to do, and I dropped to all fours, turned wolf and curled my silky fur into the man-beasts' arms.

We lay that way, the three of us, until the waning moon hung low in the sky.

## 11

The next few days at the Gordon-Scotts were busy. Adam set up state-of-the-art motion detectors, video surveillance and alarm protocols sent to a nondescript RV that sat behind the back fence near the irrigation ditch at the base of the slope. Sister Lena and crew invaded both Amber's and my territory, leaving behind the scent of burnt sage and lavender and a buzzing in my sinuses that made my nose itch. *Damn magic allergies*, I thought as I sneezed.

But it appeared to have worked. No supernatural being could cross onto our property without an invitation. Once invited, they could come and go as they pleased unless that invitation was revoked.

Sister Nayala also gave all of us humans bracelets to wear to keep out Jeanetta. And yes, collars to wear while we were turned. They were made out of nondescript leather, thank God. It would have served Jackson right if they'd given him a sparkly rainbow one, but then, he probably would have worn it with pride. Or at Pride. Whatever. Anyway, they were supposed to protect us from any of Jeanetta's attempts at possession. I wondered why they didn't just give us a charm that made all spells against us null and void, to which I got a fifteen-minute speech on the impossibilities of such a thing. And Adam lapped it up. He really did like Nayala!

Things seemed to settle after that and I was starting to feel like maybe we were out of the woods and in the clear. It was a week before Halloween and we were putting the decorations up. Halloween had become an ever-expanding tradition in the Gordon-Scott household ever since JR got old enough to trick-or-treat. Amber bought a wicker man and even a wicker witch on a broom and Elle wired them with lights to create a whimsical tableau on the front lawn.

Adam and his team created a huge blue symbol like a medicine wheel on the slope above and behind our houses. He said it was some kind of Templar thing, containing the cross and other mystical protections. The rest of Knightsbridge followed suit with decorations galore. Imagine Tim Burton designing a new part of Disneyland and you've got Knightsbridge at Halloween. No plastic knockoff decorations from those fly-by-night franchise stores that appeared in derelict malls in October. Knightsbridge's downtown looked like it had been done by the set decorator of Hocus Pocus, so much so that I kept looking for Bette Midler, Kathy Najimi and Sarah Jessica Parker to come sweeping by on vacuums. It was disturbingly beautiful, what with the leaves beginning to turn and drop and a slight nip in the air. It was California, after all, not upstate New York.

*Time to layer up,* I thought at Amber and began pulling the sweaters and boots out of storage.

*I could have told you that weeks ago,* she answered.

*Oh hey, can I borrow some candles? I'm making an altar and I know you have that PartyLite stuff from those parties you used to throw.*

Amber had spent a short time as a consultant for PartyLite Candles and Gifts, but she ate up all her profits by buying her own products. Her loss, my gain.

*You break it, you buy it,* she said.

*What?*

*You know what I mean.*

And of course I did.

I was rummaging through boxes with the garage door open, the bright white light of the garage interior beaming out into the night and drawing in the moths, much to my sister's dismay, when I heard a car door slam shut, and then the sound of heels came up the walk. I looked up from a pumpkin candleholder that looked a little like the carriage from Cinderella and saw my stepmom Rhonda standing just outside the garage, watching what I was doing with a smile.

"Amber! So good to see you."

"It's Ashlee," I sighed. The woman mixed us up half the time, and I half-believed she did so on purpose.

"Well, don't just stand there, give me a hug," she said. Though I knew such demonstrativeness was unlike her, I did. She gripped me hard for a second, then let her hands down. "You're quite athletic, aren't you, my dear?" Rhonda commented and tried to follow me back into the garage.

"Um, Ashlee?" she called as I headed to tell Amber that our Halloween houseguest had arrived. "Is there something I should know?"

I turned to watch her struggling against the spell, although it looked more like she was struggling against her suitcase.

"Oh, sorry. Come on in." I invited her in and then went to help her with her bags. Guess the step-monster had a little magic inside her after all.

*Hey Amber!* I sent over the twin bond.

*Already on it, Roz!*

Elle, JR, Ziggy, Spanky and my sister met Rhonda in the garage and ushered her into the house. Oh, right. "Athletic" me, I got to carry the bag.

Amber and Elle got Rhonda settled into the guest room. Colby ended up on my couch in the pool house and spent the evening looking for jobs on the internet. She said she loathed the idea of working on Jackson's construction crew. "I'm more of a head girl than a hands girl," she said. I wondered if she realized how that sounded.

I got my candles and put the boxes back in garage storage, and then the rest of us sat around the main house living room with our first fire of the year blazing in the hearth. Well, all except JR, who went back into his bedroom to play on whatever PlayStation or Xbox he had this year.

Rhonda didn't like dogs much, so after a few rebuffs, Spanky and Ziggy stayed over on our side of the wraparound sofa.

One fascinating thing about our stepmom, she'd spent most of her adult life as an emergency room nurse in a small town not far from Knightsbridge. She tells some real doozies about having to deliver babies when the doctor was too drunk to catch. It's quite the contradiction, because she has absolutely no bedside manner. Or maybe that was a good thing in an ER nurse, the psychic constitution of a combat field medic. Apparently her lack of empathy extends to dogs and children too. It was no big surprise that she was semi-estranged from her own adult daughters.

Amber had poured us something she called "snugglies" and I wondered if there was more kick to this potion than the usual mixture of hot chocolate and peppermint schnapps. I sniffed and savored the aroma, but I didn't sneeze, so that seemed to be a sign that the concoction was magic free.

"I thought you weren't supposed to be here till next weekend," I said to my stepmom. Open mouth, insert foot.

"Ashlee!" My twin said.

*What? You were thinking it!* I whined in her head.

*Yes, but I'd never say so out loud. You make it sound like her being here is a bad thing.* I could feel her exasperation and maybe just a little bit of amusement underneath it.

"No, she's right," Rhonda sighed. "Sorry if I've inconvenienced you. Your father is getting on my last nerve so I came early. I figured it would be easier to get forgiveness than permission."

*Well, she's right about that one,* I thought, to which Amber gave me a mental slap. Actually, it was more like dropping a cube of ice down my collar. *Hey!*

She smiled.

Okay, it was funny. I smiled too.

"Anyway, I know you must be busy. So, I'll just make myself invisible. I've been wanting to catch up on my reading anyway. It's volunteer season in Tucson and your father is busy whipping those young whippersnappers into shape. His words, not mine."

Our father "The General" organizes the volunteers who serve at the Mount Lemon Camp for Disadvantaged Boys during the winter season, which in Arizona is the nice time of year, of course. These people get free RV hookups or basic housing in return for helping the charity do its job of providing low-cost outdoor experiences for kids from all over the region.

I spied on them once when I was visiting my dad and it looked like he was having a ball ordering about those big and little soldiers. The sad part about Adam being the son that Dad always wanted is that he wanted to repeat the process with us twins, but Amber and I didn't make for good little soldiers, and he never quite got that. I know he loves us, but he never really liked us too much. It hurts, but I've come to accept it.

"Yeah, don't get between Dad and his infantry," I said, and then popped my hand over my mouth when I realized how that sounded.

Fortunately, everyone laughed.

Amber stood and asked if anyone wanted refills, but no one did. We all felt pretty tired, I think. All except for Rhonda, who sat in her chair idly twirling her index finger like she was spinning a web.

Amber said, "I've got a lot to do before the convention, but I've arranged for the Street Witches to keep you occupied until the opening ceremonies. I hear they're even doing a spiral dance Halloween night."

"Oh, I've heard of that. I think they do it in the city every All Hallow's Eve," Rhonda said and I thought it an obscure reference for someone just learning about witchcraft. I'd been dragged by my friend Xiana to it once and it was pretty powerful, even though I didn't have a witchy bone in my body. Well, okay, maybe I did, since Amber seemed to.

"So, what kind of a witch are you?" I asked.

"Ashlee!" My sister again.

"Do you mean, am I a good witch or a bad witch?" Rhonda laughed. "I guess I prefer to think of myself as neither."

*Figures*, I thought. *Methinks the woman doth protest too much.*

"I'm a solo practitioner of earth-based pueblo magic," she went on.

"Never heard of it," Amber said, voicing my thoughts exactly.

"It's a form of hearth-craft - think feng shui with Arizonan, Native American and Mexican influences. We do everything from weaving our own dreamcatchers to spinning pottery."

"So that's what the dreamcatchers are about," I said. We'd all gotten dreamcatchers for Christmas one year. I had mine hanging in the circular window on the north wall of the pool house cottage. The crystals she'd used, like teardrops on the strands of the mosaic in the centerpiece, caught the light and danced it in rainbows all over my kitchen. It made me smile at the thought.

"We channel our magic, which isn't strong enough to affect things immediately like more powerful witches can do, into household items that hold resonances of joy, warmth, comfort, acceptance and security."

"So, you're a hearth-witch," I said. The bits and pieces I'd picked up from the web said that hearth-witches were good at making people feel welcome and accepted, and though I thought she kept a nice house for my Dad, it never screamed "home" to me.

"I know I haven't been the best maternal presence in your life. I used to try more, I suppose, but after my years as an emergency room nurse and the ugliness I saw, well, let's just say I became a bit hardened to everything. Even my girls say so. This hearth-witchery helps me."

I'd forgotten about my stepsisters, Beth and Brianne. The few times we'd seen each other we'd all laughed, commiserating about our lot with our parents and stepparents who drove us nuts. We'd all felt that our respective mothers and fathers had withdrawn from us a lot when they chose to marry each other. It was only when JR was born that they started getting involved again.

"I know you don't think so much of me," Rhonda continued. "I know I could never replace your mother."

"You never even tried!" I exclaimed, shoving my foot further into my tonsils.

"Ashlee!" I could see the disapproval in Amber's frown lines.

*What? I'm sorry, but this is like the first time we've ever had a serious conversation with our stepmom without Dad being around to umpire or grunt his disapproval. Personally, I'd like to know why she's here.* I mind-butted Amber.

"No, Amber. Ashlee's right. That's one thing I think we have that's a similarity. You, Ashlee, and I. People love us or they hate us," she said.

I gave my sister a mental raspberry.

"So, why the sudden change of heart?"

"It's not a change of heart. It's me making an effort because I need to. Your father isn't doing well."

"He never said anything to me," Amber said. She talked to him more than I did. I have Daddy issues.

"Oh, he'll tell you about his physical pains, his knee replacement and his back issues. But I think your father is feeling his mortality. If it wasn't for church and the camp…" she trailed off, then cut to the chase, which is what I was about to tell her to do. "I think your father may be clinically depressed."

To the General, many of the mental illnesses diagnosed today, such as depression, are actually due to one of two things: a failure to trust in God or a lack of willpower – which is why Amber's eternal OCD and my slowly fading PTSD from killing Sean doesn't get talked about in the family. We make allowances for each other, but God forbid we should ever discuss our issues and deal with them.

"Your father will never admit it, of course," she continued.

"Maybe it's hormones," I interrupted her and Amber laughed. "No, really! Has he had his testosterone checked? Because I hear that men with low testosterone can experience ennui."

"Ennui? In layman's terms, Miss Lexicon," my twin spat.

"Lethargy or lack of anticipation for life," Rhonda said. "You may be right, which brings me to the second reason I'm here. I've heard through the grapevine there is powerful magic here in Knightsbridge. And frankly, I need more than what I can do with my minor hearth-craft to help your father." She looked over at Amber.

"There might be some herbalists I could recommend," Amber hedged. Across the twin-bond I saw a mental flash of the magic cookbook that sat on the kitchen shelf. Bet she was going to hide that soon.

"Well, all I know is that when I told a wise woman I know about what I was going through, she told me I needed to join the Street Witches association and they told me to get my carcass to a convention."

"I'll call Sister Lena in the morning. She's the head of the chapter here and I'm sure if anyone here can help you, she can," Amber said. "Now, if you don't mind…" She yawned and we all followed suit. "I'm exhausted and we can catch up more in the morning."

"Of course," my stepmother said. "Ashlee?"

"Yeah, I'm pretty tired, as well," I yawned and began to gather up our mugs and glasses to put them in the dishwasher. Amber sent me an internal thank-you on the twin line as we retired, them to bed, me to the pool house.

But not until Amber dropped a bomb on me.

*Oh, by the way, I've volunteered us to assist Con with the magic show Friday during the opening night of the Street Witches Convention. He needs identical twins to pull off the vanishing act.*

*Are you friggin' kidding me?*

*You weren't doing anything that night, were you?*

*That's not the point.*

*It's just for one trick. I go in the box on one side of the stage and you come down the aisle from the back of the auditorium; you'll be in and out in half an hour, tops.*

*I'd better,* I thought at her as I looked around my kitchenette. "I saw The Prestige and frankly I think two Scott twins is plenty."

"I'm sorry, what?" Colby said, looking up from her laptop.

"Nothing. I sometimes talk to myself. Just ignore me."

*I know I do,* Amber said and closed with, *we'll be rehearsing tomorrow, then Thursday night for dress rehearsal.*

*Oh goodie,* I sighed. So much for a half-hour commitment.

*I can't wait to see you in a rhinestone-studded thong and sparkly pasties,* Ziggy added.

"Siegfried!" My sister's voice echoed across the yard in mock outrage. At first I assumed that it was the inappropriate comment, until I got a visual of my sister's nose turning up at an awful stench.

*Ashlee, please don't feed Siegfried tofu from the stir-fry. Push it around your plate and toss it in the garbage if you don't like it, but for God's sake don't sneak it to the familiar. Gives him gas like you wouldn't believe.*

Colby looked up at me again and I shared with her how I'd given the familiar flatulence. We giggled like schoolgirls and I made us each a cup of tea as I sat down at the table to take care of correspondence I'd been neglecting.

The next day I walked in on Rhonda and Amber having a heart-to-heart. At least that's what it looked like. Elle was at work and Amber was working from home finishing up the swag bags for the convention attendees.

"I'm sure it's going to be just fine," Rhonda said, patting Amber's hand. When she pulled away, her jewelry caught on Amber's possess-me-not leather bracelet. "Oh dear," she said, reaching into her knitting bag for a pair of shears.

Before I could get in a word to prevent the disaster, Amber touched Rhonda's silver charm bangle, the snap broke open and all of the charms on her bracelet went flying onto the floor.

I reached to rescue a turtle from the rug before Spanky had it in his mouth and yelped as the thing burned me. I dropped it. I'd forgotten about the effect of silver on a werewolf. Though I wasn't normally as susceptible as a lycanthrope – yay lupine power – it appeared that my wolf being pregnant with the pups made me more vulnerable than normal.

"Are you all right, Ashlee?" my stepmom asked.

"Yeah, must have caught it on a carpet staple or something," I fudged and stuck my finger in my mouth.

Amber covered for me and Ziggy trotted over with a *let me see it* in his eyes.

I showed my boo-boo to him when Rhonda's back was turned. He licked it and surprisingly enough, it was all better. *You sure you're not a vampire?*

*Vampire, daemon. All in the same ballpark,* he replied.

Hmm.

It turned out that Con wanted to use us both for more than just one magic trick. He also wanted to saw the two of us in half and put us back together with the wrong parts, as in a box with a pair of wiggling feet stuck out of each end and another one with two heads. He'd mix them up again until we both had our feet and heads on straight. Don't ask me to reveal the secret, but it did involve smoke, mirrors, extra helpers, and hidden compartments.

One trick I thought was particularly clever was a sash and tube that went around Amber's waist, and a fake sword that had the flexibility of a contractor's measuring tape. It would look like she was being disemboweled, and to be honest, I wished I could perform more than just the illusions that demanded an identical twin.

As far as I could tell, Con wasn't doing any actual magic to perform the tricks themselves, but his expert sleight-of-hand, seductive patter and his command of suggestion and distraction would keep even a sharp witch entertained. And judging from the way my nose was itching, it was either the vanilla-scented dry ice mixture or he was using the mental vampire whammy to help things along with the audience.

Our costumes were simple fishnet stockings and high-heeled tap shoes, crowned by a unitard that kept threatening to ride up my ass like a thong, plus a tuxedo shirt, vest, and bowtie. I swear we looked like Zatana, Dr. Fate's daughter in the Justice League.

We topped off the ensemble with a top hat, tails and a cane and I got dirty looks from Amber when I kept doing a soft-shoe in the background. Shuffle-hop-step. Shuffle-ball-change. Shuffle-hop-step. Shuffle-ball-change. By the time I was through, she was ready to have me stuffed, mounted, and shuffled off to Buffalo.

Rhonda came to watch us rehearse and she gushed so much about our performance that not only did she get herself roped into being a volunteer, but she appointed herself makeup maven and costume assistant to help with a few quick-changes we had to do before the final trick where he levitated us all. Again, not going to reveal the trick, no how, no way. I can keep a secret.

Friday night soon arrived, the opening ceremonies of the convention. All the hotels, motels and airbnbs in Knightsbridge were full up, with street witches coming in from all over northern California. Main Street was expected to be packed and they closed the thoroughfare to all but foot traffic, which enabled them to use a lot of fog machines. They even hired actors to portray some of the scarier monsters from horror films.

Not being able to cruise Main was annoying, even oxymoronic, as the Street Witches were supposed to be all about keeping cruising safe, but the police figured that if people came to party, they didn't have to do it by driving up and down. The parking lots on the perimeter were filled with enough classic and customized vehicles to make a car show, though. Technically they weren't cruising if they didn't, well, cruise.

Adam had his team stationed throughout the audience at the convention center and it was a packed house. There were people from all over the country determined to keep cruising a safe part of their communities, and underneath it all, a thread of magic that threatened to make my nose itch for days.

My nerves were shot and if it hadn't been for Amber's tea of tranquility, I would have tossed my cookies then and there. As it was, I drank so much of the stuff I kept having to pee, which was so not convenient in the costumes we were wearing. At times like these, I really hated being a girl.

Other times, not so much.

Sister Lena opened the show with a welcome and a quick run-through of the agenda for the next day and a half. She warned everyone that for tonight, Main Street was open to foot traffic only, to which there were quite a few groans, but she explained that there would be a car rally and parade the next morning terminating at the local fairgrounds with a daylight offering of show cars, followed by a spiral dance at the Veterans' Memorial Hall.

"And now," she continued, "without further ado, we'd like to present the Great Shelby, a wizard in his own right, bringing astounding magic for your entertainment."

At that cue, the orchestra began a rumbling drumroll that grew in volume as a swirl of vermillion smoke poured up from the center of the stage. When it cleared, a solitary black top hat sat on the floor with a live white rabbit atop of it. Above, Con floated as if sitting on air, legs crossed in lotus position, petting a large black cat. At least I think it was a cat, I suppose it could have been somebody's familiar. It didn't smell like a shifter.

"I was wondering where I left that." Con said to the audience's delight as he unfolded his legs and stood. He moved the rabbit and the cat both to the floor. The feline took the bunny by the scruff of its neck like a kitten and loped off-stage. "Don't worry," he told the audience, "I've raised those two together since they were born." Then he picked up his hat and Amber's head appeared under it.

"Mr. Shelby, I think you forgot something," she said and he laughed.

He put the top hat back down over her head before backing up and taking his foot to it as if he were kicking a soccer goal. The hat exploded in a shower of confetti and I was suddenly lit by follow-spot, sitting above him on a half-moon, as if he'd kicked Amber across the room.

The audience cheered as Shelby moved a rolling ladder into place and helped me descend to the floor. "Ladies and Gentleman, my assistant, Ms. Scott."

The rest of the tricks rolled out as planned: floating zombie balls, juggling zombie heads, assistants vanishing and reappearing, even some mind-reading. After a particularly disturbing blackout illusion where I walked around in the same costume as Amber with a hood over my head as her disembodied head seemed to float behind me while ghosts, ghouls and goblins took up residence in the audience, I ran backstage for Amber's last costume change.

"Amber dear, I don't know how to tell you this," Rhonda whispered as Con mesmerized the audience and did a few mind whammies on them with his vampire powers, "but your zipper's stuck and I can't get it undone."

I went to try to help, but it was useless.

"Ashlee, you're going to have to go on for me," Amber said, pushing a costume into my hands. Of course, trooper that I am, I began donning the costume. The show must go on, after all!

Rhonda wrapped the sash and tube around me and I realized that I was getting to do a trick I'd been envious of anyway, the one with the flexible fake sword. Amber pouted, but she was being a good sport about it. She shoved me onstage and watched from the wings as Con motioned to me.

"Ah, Miss Scott, there you are," he said. He had just finished showing the audience the sword that he was theoretically going to plunge into me – the real one, not the one that we used for the trick.

I took the sword from him and placed it in the colorful metal canister he'd been using to pull objects from all night long.

"And how fortunate," he said, "that tonight, to help me with this trick, we have your own stepmother, Rhonda Scott, to assist you."

I guess this was the trick she'd volunteered for.

"I truly hope this isn't payback for calling her a step-monster," he said melodramatically, and the audience laughed.

Rhonda strode out onstage, confident as could be, grabbed the sword from the canister and came toward me. Con was making a show of instructing her where to position the sword and asked the audience to count with him as he made airy-fairy hand gestures as she got ready to put the trick sword into me. The drums began to roll as the audience counted down.

"Three! Two! One!" they called, and before the push, I heard Amber scream and come running on stage, to the delight of the audience. They must have thought it was part of the act.

I looked up at her, my brow wrinkling, opened up the twin bond wide, but only felt fear and terror in her heart. I looked from her and then into Rhonda's face, twisted with unexpected hatred.

With the force of a pile driver she shoved the silver sword through my body and out the other side. Silver! The pain was so great, I doubled over in shock and felt something vital rupture around the blade. The silver burned and I recoiled against the agony, straightening my body again.

I could see the horror on Con's face and the audience whooped with delight, still convinced this was all in fun. The vampire's fangs came out as blood stained my costume and dripped down my thighs.

Rhonda stepped back in triumph and crowed. I saw the spirit of Jeanetta Macdonald rising out of her body, and then my stepmom dropped like a stone. I seemed frozen in place, upright but barely conscious.

"No!" Amber ran toward me.

Con stepped forward, snapped his fingers, and the audience froze, except for Lena, Nayala and the inner circle of the coven. I guess I could drop the "Sister," since it appeared that I was dying; we might as well be on a first-name basis.

Adam ran in from the opposite side of the stage where he had been watching the show. His team took up positions in front of the stage. "Nayala! Stasis spell! Lena!" he cried, but Lena was already chanting.

*Numb these wounds from stem to stern*
*Stem the blood flow in the urn*
*Hold this lupine timeless*
*From the consequences of this violence*

Not a bad rhyme, made up on the spot as it was. Mercifully, I couldn't feel anything. I could turn my head. I could see, and hear and speak, but as far as the rest of my body was concerned, I was paralyzed.

Before I knew it, I was surrounded by the pack. The lycanthropes yipped and vocalized and I could feel pack magic supporting me, buoying me against the tide of pain I knew would catch up with me. The witches were chanting as well and I was being held by Con's intimates who had been working backstage as stagehands.

The audience remained frozen, minds held by the power of Con's magic. The next thing I saw was Will's face and then Jackson's pressing next to mine. Sully's face captured my attention, wavering like smoke before my eyes.

"We've got you Ashlee," Sully said. "But I'm afraid it's punctured something vital."

The pups? No, they shouldn't even be there when I was in human form, right? *Oh, God, please let it be so.*

Above the smell of blood came the aroma of rotting putridness, of sewage and bile. And if I'd had the stomach for it, pardon the pun, I'd have hurled.

Then Con was moving in; he'd slid up his sleeve and used his fangs to puncture his own arm, and his thick vampire blood quivered heavy in the wound.

"No!" I yelled at him.

"Ashlee, he has to," Adam said, taking Sully's place in my limited view. "Otherwise we can't take the sword out. The werewolves can't touch it and the witches can only keep you in stasis for so long. I can purify the injury, but Con's blood is the only thing that can save you for sure."

"No blood debt," I growled at him and turned my head to Con. "You hear me. No blood debt. I know how you work, and I owe you nothing. This is your choice."

"You owe me nothing."

"And neither does my family."

"I absolve you of all obligations, for you and all of your family. I'm doing this for purely selfish reasons. I need my pack intact."

"Pack included," I added.

He hesitated at this, and then sighed.

"Fine. Pack included," he said, then shoved his bleeding wrist into my mouth. "Suck it."

I sucked, and no, it's not so erotic when it goes the other way.

"I'm not going to lie to you, Ash," Adam said. "This is gonna hurt." In one fell swoop, without any more warning, Adam slid the sword out of me while Will and Jackson held my shoulders. If I thought the damn thing hurt going in, it was ten times worse coming out.

Adam placed his one hand on my sternum and the other on my back. Where he touched, the blood disappeared as if absorbed by his skin, and his hands began to glow. My brain went a little loopy for a moment as I tried not to retch from the taste of copper pennies in my mouth. I could feel my insides rearrange as the stasis slipped off me.

"Enough!" Con yanked his arm from my bloodstained mouth, licked his arm clean and rolled his shirtsleeve back down. The pack caught me before I hit the floor.

Will propped me up against his chest and I saw Elle standing onstage with her arms around my sister and Colby behind them looking helpless.

With help from Jackson, Sully and Adam I managed to stand, and though my body was tingling, it felt perfectly whole. In fact, better than whole. I felt like I'd run a marathon, won the damn thing and had energy to spare. *Damn, vampire blood is powerful,* I thought, then wondered about the side effects. Guess I'd have to ask the Con-man later.

A couple of Adam's men mounted the stage and proceeded to pick Rhonda up off the floor and carry her past Colby, who took one look at her, snarled and said, "I hate stepmothers."

That made me bust out laughing, a stress-relief response, I guess.

Amber and Elle rushed over and we all hugged. I motioned to Colby and she joined us. We held each other for a moment until it got awkward and we all let go.

"What's going to happen to her?" I asked Adam as his men made their way out of the auditorium with Rhonda's comatose body.

"Knightsbridge General," he said. "I'll call Dad."

"Why bother him? It wasn't Rhonda, really. It was Jeanetta again. We really have to take care of that bitch."

Adam stared at me. "You keep using pointless euphemisms. She'll never stop until she's dead."

"What if she's more powerful when she'd dead?" I asked. "Like Ghost Mom?"

He looked sour. "Good point. But something needs to be done."

"Agreed."

"I'll call Samantha, tell her what's coming," Will said, but before he did, he took me in his arms and kissed me.

I melted. I truly melted, like I hadn't in a while, since he'd gotten all testostero-PMS-y. If I hadn't known he was the right man for me before, I did now. He may not be the pack's alpha, but he was mine.

"Ahem," Con muttered, and I glanced at him. Then I looked around the room and realized we had an audience still in mental thrall to take care of.

"The show must go on," he said, and he sent all his helpers offstage and back to their seats. He pulled Amber and me aside and said, "Just follow my lead," and then he turned to the audience, rewound the debacle out of their heads and when he snapped his fingers, followed up with a levitation spell and a silhouette play where he turned from wolf to crow to owl to mist, and then appeared at the edge of the stage while he blanked the spectators' minds of the horror of the whole incident.

"Ladies and Gentlemen, thank you for coming and I want to give a special thanks to my assistants, Amber and Ashlee Scott." As one we walked forward, taking his hands. "Enjoy the rest of your convention." He raised our hands and we took a bow and walked off to thundering applause.

# −12−

After checking Rhonda into Knightsbridge General, we all gathered in a corner of the hospital cafeteria: Elle, Amber, Colby, me, the pack, the witches, Adam, Con, and Will's mother Peg, Will's mom, everybody. We more or less took over the place, but there weren't many other people there right then.

Though the vampire and Peg's match-up was still disturbing, I couldn't exactly judge now, could I? I mean, they were no weirder than we were. Or, not much, anyway.

Peg smiled at me as if we shared a secret. After all, I had Con's blood running through my veins as well, for a while.

Sister Lena got on the phone to Chowchilla Women's Correctional Facility and it appeared that Jeanetta had woken up from her coma, beaming. The witch reported that before Jeanetta had a chance to say a word, one of their insiders shot her up with a powerful antipsychotic drug and she was placed in an isolation ward. Sister Nayala was even now gathering a group of witches to converge on the prison to bind her powers permanently.

After I heard this, the dialogue of *The Craft* ran through my head, only substituting Jeanetta's name for Fairuza Balk's character Nancy. *I bind you Jeanetta, from doing harm to others, and yourself.* At least that's how I think it went.

"You're sure this is gonna work?" I asked. "Permanently?"

"Yes, dear," Lena sighed. "It's drastic, but necessary."

"You sure we don't just wanna kill her?" Will interjected.

*That's my alpha,* I thought.

Amber pursed her lips. The rest of them had the decency to seem uncomfortable, but I knew how they felt.

"Hey Ashlee, can I talk to you?" Will took my hand, pulling me out of my chair as the group made idle chitchat and nursed their mocha cappuccinos.

He led me across the linoleum to the floor-to-ceiling windows that looked out over the sparkling lights of Knightsbridge, our reflections wavering in the glass. He took my hands, looked into my eyes and said, "Ashlee Scott, I love you."

I began to cry. Oh, hell, I sobbed. As he held me, the waves of tension that I'd been under since this whole thing started rolled out of me. He knelt and pressed his face into my belly, then grabbed me around the waist as I slid to the floor next to him, cry-snot pouring from my nose. I know, attractive, right? He handed me a cotton handkerchief and I blew.

Thank God for old-fashioned men with pocket hankies. Then I folded it up and handed it back to him. Yuck.

With my nose red and running, my eyes brimming with tears, he braved the terror of my mucked-up face. Took my chin in one hand, tilted his head and kissed me. His lips were soft and tender. They were everything I ever wanted and I could hear his heart pound. I put a hand upon his chest and pushed, breaking the contact.

"I look horrible," I told him, turning my head.

"I don't care."

I looked into his eyes and I knew his words were true. "Why now? Is this just foreplay? Another brush with death turning you on?"

"I didn't brush with death, you did."

"Oh, yeah."

He kissed me again and when we came up for air, his eyes brimmed with tears. I felt a little tap on my sternum and looked down to see a diamond ring sparkling in a blue velvet box. And then, he asked me the question I'd been waiting to hear all of my life. The question, I thought, that I would never hear when I found out I was a werewolf.

"Ashlee Marie Scott, will you marry me?"

"Here? On the floor by the window, with no one around?"

"I wanted to make sure you'd say yes first."

"Chickenshit." I stood up and dragged him to his feet, pointing over to where our friends sat on plastic chairs at plastic tables in a plastic cafeteria. Oh, well, it could be worse. "Do it right."

Will took my hand and led me over to the others, who all turned to stare as he dropped to a knee. "Ashlee Marie Scott, will you marry me?" he said again.

What could I say but yes?

And I felt my mother's arms materialize around me as she became visible to us all.

Suddenly I was swarmed by sisters and brothers. Again, it occurred to me what life was all about. It was family. Born of blood, sweat or tears, chosen or not, family was what made all the insanity make sense.

Sure, Rhonda was in a coma and my dad was on his way. But those were problems for another day. At least tonight. *Or I should say, today?* I thought as the sun slipped over the horizon. Today, I was going to accept the love around me.

Today, I was an unreserved yes. And the rest of the world could go – well, you know.

## THE END of BLOODMOON

**Sign up for David VanDyke's Exclusive Insiders Group at:**
**www.davidvandykeauthor.com**

32526015R00120

Made in the USA
Middletown, DE
05 January 2019